The Fall of the Year

This edition published 2025
by Living Book Press
Copyright © Living Book Press, 2025

ISBN: 978-1-76153-885-8 (hardcover)
         978-1-76153-911-4 (softcover)

First published in 1911.

A catalogue record for this book is available from the National Library of Australia

The Fall of the Year

by

Dallas Lore Sharp

"ONE OF THE EAGLES STRUCK ME A STINGING BLOW ON THE HEAD"

Contents

NOTE

It is interesting to observe that the subject of the initial for chapter IV is witch-hazel; that for chapter VII, the cocoons of the cecropia, the promethea, and the basket worm; and that for chapter VIII, a sprig of alder, with the old fruit and a budded catkin. The subjects of the other initials require no identification.

INTRODUCTION

There are three serious charges brought against nature books of the present time, namely, that they are either so dull as to be unreadable, or so fanciful as to be misleading, or so insincere as to be positively harmful. There is a real bottom to each of these charges.

Dull nature-writing is the circumstantial, the detailed, the cataloguing, the semi-scientific sort, dried up like old Rameses and cured for all time with the fine-ground spice of measurements, dates, conditions—observations, so called. For literary purposes, one observation of this kind is better than two. Rarely does the watcher in the woods see anything so new that for itself it is worth recording. It is not what one sees, so much as the manner of the seeing, not the observation but its suggestions that count for interest to the reader. Science wants the exact observation; nature-writing wants the observation exact and the heart of the observer along with it. We want plenty of facts in our nature books, but they have all been set down in order before; what has not been set down before are the author's thoughts and emotions. These should be new, personal, and are pretty sure therefore to be interesting.

More serious than dullness (and that is serious enough) is the charge that nature books are untrustworthy, that they falsify the facts, and give a wrong impression of nature. Some nature books do, as some novels do with the facts of human life. A nature book all full of extraordinary, better-class animals who do extraordinary stunts because of their superior powers has little of real nature in it. There are no such extraordinary animals, they do no such extraordinary things. Nature is full of marvels—Niagara Falls, a flying swallow, a star, a ragweed, a pebble; but nature is not full of dragons and centaurs and foxes that reason like men and take their tea with lemon, if you please.

I have never seen one of these extraordinary animals, never saw anything extraordinary out of doors, because the ordinary is so surprisingly marvelous. And I have lived in the woods practically all of my life. And you will never see one of them—a very good argument against anybody's having seen them.

The world out of doors is not a circus of performing prodigies, nor are nature-writers strange half-human creatures who know wood-magic, who talk with trees, and call the birds and beasts about them as did one of the saints of old. No, they are plain people, who have seen nothing more wonderful in the woods than you have, if they would tell the truth.

When I protested with a popular nature-writer some time ago at one of his exciting but utterly impossible fox stories, he wrote back,—

"The publishers demanded that chapter to make the book sell."

Now the publishers of this book make no such demands. Indeed they have had an expert naturalist and woodsman hunting up and down every line of this book for errors of fact, false suggestions, wrong sentiments, and extraordinaries of every sort. If this book is not exciting it is the publishers' fault. It may not be exciting, but I believe, and hope, that it is *true* to all of my out of doors, and not untrue to any of yours.

The charge of insincerity, the last in the list, concerns the author's style and sentiments. It does not belong in the same category with the other two, for it really includes them. Insincerity is the mother of all the literary sins. If the writer cannot be true to himself, he cannot be true to anything. Children are the particular victims of the evil. How often are children spoken to in baby-talk, gush, hollow questions, and a condescension as irritating as coming teeth! They are written to, also, in the same spirit.

The temptation to sentimentalize in writing of the "beauties of nature" is very strong. Raptures run through nature books as regularly as barbs the length of wire fences. The world according to such books is like the Garden of Eden according to Ridinger, all peace, in spite of the monstrous open-jawed alligator in the foreground of the picture, who must be smiling, I take it, in an alligatorish way at a fat swan near by.

Just as strong to the story-writer is the temptation to blacken the shadows of the picture—to make all life a tragedy. Here on my table lies a child's nature-book every chapter of which ends in death—nothing but struggle to escape for a brief time the bloody jaws of the bigger beast—or of the superior beast, man.

Neither extreme is true of nature. Struggle and death go on, but, except where man interferes, a very even balance is maintained, peace prevails over fear, joy lasts longer than pain, and life continues to multiply and replenish the earth. "The level of wild life," to quote my words from "The Face of the Fields," "of the soul of all nature is a great serenity. It is seldom lowered, but often raised to a higher level, intenser, faster, more exultant."

This is a divinely beautiful world, a marvelously interesting world, the best conceivable sort of a world to live in, notwithstanding its gypsy moths, tornadoes, and germs, its laws of gravity, and of cause and effect; and my purpose in this series of nature books is to help my readers to come by this belief. A clear understanding of the laws of the Universe will be necessary for such a belief in the end, and with the understanding a profound faith in their perfect working together. But for the present, in these books of the Seasons, if I can describe the out of doors, its living creatures and their doings, its winds and skies with their suggestions—all of the out of doors, as it surrounds and supports me here in my home on Mullein Hill, Hingham, so that you can see how your out of doors surrounds and supports you, with all its manifold life and beauty, then I have done enough. If only I can accomplish a fraction of this I have done enough.

DALLAS LORE SHARP.
MULLEIN HILL, September, 1911.

THE FALL OF THE YEAR

THE CLOCK STRIKES ONE

"The clock strikes one,
    And all is still around the house!
But in the gloom
    A little mouse
Goes creepy-creep from room to room."

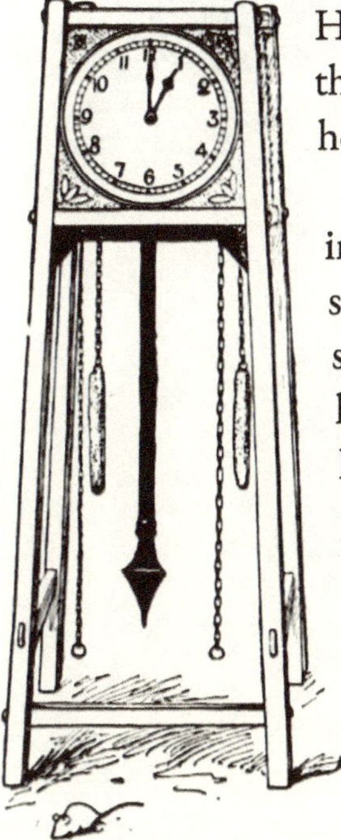

HE clock of the year strikes one!—not in the dark silent night of winter, but in the hot light of midsummer.

It is a burning July day,—one o'clock in the afternoon of the year,—and all is still around the fields and woods. All is still. All is hushed. But yet, as I listen, I hear things in the dried grass, and in the leaves overhead, going "creepy-creep," as you have heard the little mouse in the silent night.

I am lying on a bed of grass in the shade of a great oak tree, as the clock of the year strikes one. I am all alone in the quiet of the hot, hushed day. Alone? Are you alone in the big upstairs at midnight, when you hear the little mouse going "creepy-creep" from room to room? No; and I am not alone.

High overhead the clouds are drifting past; and between them, far away, is the blue of the sky—and how blue, how cool, how far, far away! But how near and warm seems the earth!

I lie outstretched upon it, feeling the burnt crisp grass beneath me, a beetle creeping under my shoulder, the heat of a big stone against my side. I throw out my hands, push my fingers into the hot soil, and try to take hold of the big earth as if I were a child clinging to my mother.

And so I am. But I am not frightened, as I used to be, when the little mouse went "creepy-creep," and my real mother brought a candle to scare the mouse away. It is because I am growing old? But I cannot grow old to my mother. And the earth is my mother, my second mother. The beetle moving under my shoulder is one of my brothers; the hot stone by my side is another of my brothers; the big oak tree over me is another of my brothers; and so are the clouds, the white clouds drifting, drifting, drifting, so far away yonder, through the blue, blue sky.

The clock of the year strikes one. The summer sun is overhead. The flood-tide of summer life has come. It is the noon hour of the year.

The drowsy silence of the full, hot noon lies deep across the field. Stream and cattle and pasture-slope are quiet in repose. The eyes of the earth are heavy. The air is asleep. Yet the round shadow of my oak begins to shift. The cattle do not move; the pasture still sleeps under the wide, white glare.

But already the noon is passing—to-day I see the signs of coming autumn everywhere.

Of the four seasons of the year summer is the shortest, and

the one we are least acquainted with. Summer is hardly a pause between spring and autumn, simply the hour of the year's noon.

We can be glad with the spring, sad with the autumn, eager with the winter; but it is hard for us to go softly, to pause and to be still with the summer; to rest on our wings a little like the broad-winged hawk yonder, far up in the wide sky.

But now the hawk is not still. The shadow of my oak begins to lengthen. The hour is gone; and, wavering softly down the languid air, falls a yellow leaf from a slender birch near by. I remember, too, that on my way through the woodlot I frightened a small flock of robins from a pine; and more than a week ago the swallows were gathering upon the telegraph wires. So quickly summer passes. It was springtime but yesterday, it seems; to-day the autumn is here.

It is a July day. At dawn the birds were singing, fresh and full-throated almost as in spring. Then the sun burned through the mist, and the chorus ceased. Now I do not hear even the chewink and the talkative vireo. Only the fiery notes of the scarlet tanager come to me through the dry white heat of the noon, and the resonant song of the indigo bunting—a hot, metallic, quivering song, as out of a "hot and copper sky."

There are nestlings still in the woods. This indigo bunting has eggs or young in the bushes of the hillside; the scarlet tanager by some accident has but lately finished his nest in the tall oaks. I looked in upon some half-fledged cuckoos along the fence. But all of these are late. Most of the year's young are upon the wing.

A few of the spring's flowers are still opening. I noticed the bees upon some tardy raspberry blossoms; here and there is a stray dandelion. But these are late. The season's fruit has already set, is already ripening. Spring is gone; the sun is overhead; the red wood-lily is open. To-day is the noon of the year.

High noon! and the red wood-lily is aflame in the old fields, and in the low tangles of sweet-fern and blackberry that border the upland woods.

The wood-lily is the flower of fire. How impossible it would be to kindle a wood-lily on the cold, damp soil of April! It can be lighted only on this kiln-dried soil of July. This old hilly pasture is baking in the sun; the low mouldy moss that creeps over its thin breast crackles and crumbles under my feet; the patches of sweet-fern that blotch it here and there crisp in the heat and fill the smothered air with their spicy breath; while the wood-lily opens wide and full, lifting its spotted lips to the sun for his scorching kiss. See it glow! Should the withered thicket burst suddenly into a blaze, it would be no wonder, so hot and fiery seem the petals of this flower of the sun.

How unlike the tender, delicate fragrant flowers of spring are these strong flowers of the coming fall! They make a high bank along the stream—milkweed, boneset, peppermint, turtle-head, joe-pye-weed, jewel-weed, smartweed, and budding goldenrod! Life has grown lusty and lazy and rank.

But life has to grow lusty and rank, for the winter is coming; and as the woodchucks are eating and eating, enough to last them until spring comes again, so the plants are storing fat in their tap-roots, and ripening millions of seeds, to carry them safely through the long dead months of winter.

The autumn is the great planting time out of doors. Every autumn wind is a sower going forth to sow. And he must have seeds and to spare—seeds for the waysides for the winter birds to eat, seeds for the stony places where there is no depth of soil for them, seeds for the ploughed fields where they are not allowed to grow, seeds for every nook and corner, in order that somewhere each plant may find a place to live, and so continue its kind from year to year.

Look at the seeds of the boneset, joe-pye-weed, milkweed, and goldenrod! Seeds with wings and plumes and parachutes that go floating and flying and ballooning.

> "Over the fields where the daisies grow,
>   Over the flushing clover,
> A host of the tiniest fairies go—
> Dancing, balancing to and fro,
>   Rolling and tumbling over.
>
> "Quivering, balancing, drifting by,
>   Floating in sun and shadow—
> Maybe the souls of the flowers that die
> Wander, like this, to the summer sky
>   Over a happy meadow."

So they do. They wander away to the sky, but they come down again to the meadow to make it happy next summer with new flowers; for these are the seed-souls of thistles and daisies and fall dandelions seeking new bodies for themselves in the warm soil of Mother Earth.

Mother Earth! How tender and warm and abundant she is! As I lie here under the oak, a child in her arms, I see the thistle-down go floating by, and on the same laggard breeze comes up from the maple swamp the odor of the sweet pepper-bush. A little flock of chickadees stop in the white birches and quiz me. "Who are you?" "Who are you-you-you?" they ask, dropping down closer and closer to get a peek into my face.

Perhaps they don't know who I am. Perhaps I don't know

who they are. They are not fish hawks, of course; but neither am I an alligator or a pumpkin, as the chickadees surely know. This much I am quite sure of, however: that this little flock is a family—a family of young chickadees and their two parents, it may be, who are out seeing the world together, and who will stay together far into the cold coming winter.

They are one of the first signs of the autumn to me, and one of my surest, sweetest comforts as the bleak cold winds come down from the north. For the winds will not drive my chickadees away, no matter how cold and how hard they blow, no matter how dark and how dead the winter woods when, in the night of the year, the clock strikes twelve.

The clock to-day strikes one, and all is still with drowsy sleep out of doors. The big yellow butterflies, like falling leaves, are flitting through the woods; the thistledown is floating, floating past; and in the sleepy air I see the shimmering of the spiders' silky balloons, as the tiny aeronauts sail over on their strange voyages through the sky.

How easy to climb into one of their baskets, and in the fairy craft drift far, far away! How pleasant, too, if only the noon of the year would last and last; if only the warm sun would shine and shine; if only the soft sleepy winds would sleep and sleep; if only we had nothing to do but drift and drift and drift!

But we have a great deal to do, and we can't get any of it done by drifting. Nor can we get it done by lying, as I am lying, outstretched upon the warm earth this July day. Already the sun has passed overhead; already the cattle are up and grazing; already the round shadow of the oak tree begins to lie long across the slope. The noon hour is spent. I hear the quivering click-clack of a mowing-machine in a distant hay field. The work of the day goes on. My hour of rest is almost over, my summer vacation is nearly done. Work begins again to-morrow.

But I am ready for it. I have rested outstretched upon the warm earth. I have breathed the sweet air of the woods. I have felt the warm life-giving sun upon my face. I have been a child of the earth. I have been a brother to the stone and the bird and the beetle. And now I am strong to do my work, no matter what it is.

CHAPTER II
ALONG THE HIGHWAY
OF THE FOX

ITH only half a chance our smaller wild animals—the fox, the mink, the 'coon, the 'possum, the rabbit— would thrive, and be happy forever on the very edges of the towns and cities. Instead of a hindrance, houses and farms, roads and railways are a help to the wild animals, affording them food and shelter as their natural con- ditions never could. So, at least, it seems; for here on Mullein Hill, hardly twenty miles from the heart of Boston, there are more wild animals than I know what to do with—just as if the city of Boston were a big skunk farm or fox farm, from which the countryside all around (particularly my countryside) were being continually restocked.

But then, if I seem to have more foxes than a man of chickens needs to have, it is no wonder, living as I do on a main traveled road in Foxland, a road that begins off in the granite ledges this side of Boston, no one knows where, and, branching, doubling, turning, no one knows how many times, comes down at last along the trout brook to the street in front of my house, where, leaping the brook and crossing the street, it runs beside my foot-path, up the hill, to the mowing-field behind the barn.

When I say that last fall the hunters, standing near the brook where this wild-animal road and the wagon road cross, shot seven foxes, you will be quite ready to believe that this is a much-traveled road, this road of the foxes that cuts across my mowing-field; and also that I am quite likely to see the travelers, now and then, as they pass by.

So I am, especially in the autumn, when game grows scarce; when the keen frosty air sharpens the foxes' appetites, and the dogs, turned loose in the woods, send the creatures far and wide for—chickens!

For chickens? If you have chickens, I hope your chicken-coop does not stand along the side of a fox road, as mine does. For straight across the mowing-field runs this road of the foxes, then in a complete circle right round the chicken yard, and up the bushy ridge into the wood.

How very convenient! Very, indeed! And how thoughtful of me! Very thoughtful! The foxes appreciate my kindness; and they make a point of stopping at the hen-yard every time they pass this way.

It is interesting to know, too, that they pass this way almost every night, and almost every afternoon, and at almost every other odd time, so that the hens, with hundreds of grubby acres to scratch in, have to be fenced within a bare narrow yard, where they can only be *seen* by the passing foxes.

Even while being driven by the dogs, when naturally they are in something of a hurry, the foxes will manage to get far enough ahead of the hounds to come by this way and saunter leisurely around the coop.

I have a double-barreled gun and four small boys; but terrible as that combination sounds, it fails somehow with the foxes. It is a two-barreled-four-boyed kind of a joke to them. They think that I am fooling when I blaze away with both barrels at them. But I am not. Every cartridge is loaded with BB shot. But that only means *Blank-Blank* to them, in spite of all I can do. The way they jump when the gun goes off, then stop and look at me, is very irritating.

This last spring I fired twice at a fox, who jumped as if I had hit him (I must have hit him), then turned himself around and looked all over the end of the barn to see where the shots were coming from. They were coming from the back barn window, as he saw when I yelled at him.

It was an April morning, cold and foggy, so cold and foggy and so very early that my chattering teeth, I think, disturbed my aim.

It must have been about four o'clock when one of the small boys tiptoed into my room and whispered, "Father, quick! there's a fox digging under Pigeon Henny's coop behind the barn."

I was up in a second, and into the boys' room. Sure enough, there in the fog of the dim morning I could make out the moving form of a fox. He was digging under the wire runway of the coop.

The old hen was clucking in terror to her chicks. It was she who had awakened the boys.

There was no time to lose. Downstairs I went, down into the basement, where I seized the gun, and, slipping in a couple of shells, slid out of the cellar door and crept stealthily into the barn.

The back window was open. The thick wet fog poured in like dense smoke. I moved swiftly in my bare feet and peered down upon the field. There stood the blur of the coop,—a dark shadow only in the fog,—but where was the fox?

Pushing the muzzle of my double-barreled gun across the window-sill, I waited. And there in the mist stood the fox, reaching in with his paw under the wire that inclosed the coop.

Carefully, deliberately, I swung the gun on the window-sill until the bead drew dead upon the thief; then, fixing myself as firmly as I could with bare feet, I made sure of my mark and fired.

I do not wonder that the fox jumped. I jumped, myself, as both barrels went off together. A gun is a sudden thing at any time of day, but so early in the morning, and when everything was wrapped in silence and ocean fog, the double explosion was extremely startling.

The fox jumped, as naturally he would. When, however, he turned deliberately around and looked all over the end of the barn to see where I was firing from, and stood there, until I shouted at him—I say it was irritating.

But I was glad, on going out later, to find that neither charge of shot had hit the coop. The coop was rather large, larger than the ordinary coop; and taking that into account, and the thick, uncertain condition of the atmosphere, I had not made a bad shot after all. It was something not to have killed the hen.

But the fox had killed eleven of the chicks. One out of the brood of twelve was left. The rascal had dug a hole under the wire; and then, by waiting as they came out, or by frightening them out, had eaten them one by one.

There are guns and guns, and some, I know, that shoot

straight. But guns and dogs and a dense population have not yet availed here against the fox.

One might think, however, when the dogs are baying hard on the heels of a fox, that one's chickens would be safe enough for the moment from that particular fox. But there is no pack of hounds hunting in these woods swift enough or keen enough to match the fox. In literature the cunning of the fox is very greatly exaggerated. Yet it is, in fact, more than equal to that of the hound.

A fox, I really believe, enjoys an all-day run before the dogs. And as for house dogs, I have seen a fox, that was evidently out for mischief and utterly tired of himself, come walking along the edge of the knoll here by the house, and, squatting on his haunches, yap down lonesomely at the two farm dogs below.

This very week I heard the hounds far away in the ledges. I listened. They were coming toward me, and apparently on my side of the brook. I had just paused at the corner of the barn when the fox, slipping along the edge of the woods, came loping down to the hen-yard within easy gun-shot of me. He halted for a hungry look at the hens through the wire fence, then trotted slowly off, with the dogs yelping fully five minutes away in the swamp.

How many minutes would it have taken that fox to snatch a hen, had there been a hen on *his* side of the fence? He could have made chicken-sandwiches of a hen in five minutes, could have eaten them, too, and put the feathers into a bolster—almost! How many of my hens he has made into pie in less than five minutes!

As desserts go, out of doors, he has a right to a pie for fooling the dogs out of those five crowded minutes. For he does it against such uneven odds, and does it so neatly—sometimes so very thrillingly! On three occasions I have seen him do the trick, each time by a little different dodge.

One day, as I was climbing the wooded ridge behind the farm, I heard a single foxhound yelping at intervals in the hollow beyond. Coming cautiously to the top, I saw the hound below me beating slowly along through the bare sprout-land, half a mile away, and having a hard time holding to the trail. Every few minutes he would solemnly throw his big black head into the air, stop stock-still, and yelp a long doleful yelp, as if begging the fox to stop its fooling and try to leave a reasonable trail.

The hound was walking, not running; and round and round he would go, off this way, off that, then back when, catching the scent again, he would up with his muzzle and howl for all the woods to hear. But I think it was for the fox to hear.

I was watching the curious and solemn performance, and wondering if the fox really did hear and understand, when, not far from me, on the crown of the ridge, something stirred.

Without moving so much as my eyes, I saw the fox, a big beauty, going slowly and cautiously round and round in a small circle among the bushes, then straight off for a few steps, then back in the same tracks; off again in another direction and back again; then in and out, round and round, until, springing lightly away from the top of a big stump near by, the wily creature went gliding swiftly down the slope.

The hound with absolute patience worked his sure way up the hill to the circle and began to go round and round, sniffling and whimpering to himself, as I now could hear; sniffling and whimpering with impatience, but true to every foot-print of the trail. Round and round, in and out, back and forth, he went, but each time in a wider circle, until the real trail was picked up, and he was away with an eager cry.

I once again saw the trick played, so close to me, and so deliberately, with such cool calculating, that it came with something of a revelation to me of how the fox may feel, of what may be the state of mind in the wild animal world.

It was a late October evening, crisp and clear, with a moon almost full. I had come up from the meadow to the edge of the field behind the barn, and stood leaning back upon a short-handled hayfork, looking. It was at everything that I was looking—the moonlight, the gleaming grass, the very stillness, so real and visible it seemed at the falling of this first frost. I was listening too, when, as far away as the stars, it seemed, came the cry of the hounds.

You have heard at night the passing of a train beyond the mountains? the sound of thole-pins round a distant curve in the river? the closing of a barn door somewhere down the valley? Strange it may seem to one who has never listened, but the far-off cry of the hounds is another such friendly and human voice, calling across the vast of the night.

They were coming. How clear their tones, and bell-like! How mellow in the distance, ringing on the rim of the moonlit sky, as round the sides of a swinging silver bell. Their clanging tongues beat all in unison, the sound rising and falling through the rolling woodland, and spreading like a curling wave as the pack broke into the open over the level meadows.

I waited. Rounder, clearer, came the cry. I began to pick out the individual voices as now this one, now that, led the chorus across some mighty measure of The Chase.

Was it a twig that broke? Some brittle oak leaf that cracked in

"OVER THE HILL IN A WHIRLWIND OF DUST AND HOWLS"

the path behind me? A soft sound of feet! Something breathed, stopped, came on—and in the moonlight before me stood the fox!

The dogs were coming, but I was standing still. And who was I, anyway? A stump? A post? No, he saw instantly that I was more than an ordinary post. How much more?

The dogs were coming!

"Well," said he, as plainly as anything was ever said, "I don't know what you are. But I will find out." And up he came and sniffed at my shoes. "This is odd," he went on, backing carefully off and sitting down on his tail in the edge of a pine-tree shadow. "Odd indeed. Not a stump; not a man, in spite of appearances, for a man could never stand still so long as that."

The dogs were crashing through the underbrush below, their fierce cries quivering through the very trees about me.

The fox got up, trotted back and forth in front of me for the best possible view, muttering, "Too bad! Too bad! What an infernal nuisance a pack of poodles can make of themselves at times! Here is something new in the woods, and smells of the hen-yard, as I live! Those silly dogs!" and trotting back, down the path over which he had just come, he ran directly toward the coming hounds, leaped off into a pile of brush and stones, and vanished as the hounds rushed up in a yelping, panting whirl about me.

Cool? Indeed it was! He probably did not stop, as soon as he was out of sight, and make faces at the whole pack. But that is because they have politer ways in Foxland.

It is no such walking-match as this every time. It is nip and tuck, neck and neck, a dead heat sometimes, when only his superior knowledge of the ground saves the fox a whole skin.

Perhaps there are peculiar conditions, at times, that are harder for the fox than for the dogs, as when the undergrowth is all adrip with rain or dew, and every jump forward is like a plunge overboard. His red coat is longer than the short, close hair of the hound, and his big brush of a tail, heavy with water, must be a dragging weight over the long hard course of the hunt. If wet fur to him means the same as wet clothes to us, then the narrow escape I witnessed a short time ago is easily explained. It happened in this way:—

I was out in the road by the brook when I caught the cry of the pack; and, hurrying up the hill to the "cut," I climbed the gravel bank for a view down the road each way, not knowing along which side of the brook the chase was coming, nor where the fox would cross.

Not since the Flood had there been a wetter morning. The air could not stir without spilling; the leaves hung weighted with the wet; the very cries of the hounds sounded thick and choking, as the pack floundered through the alder swamp that lay at the foot of the hill where I was waiting.

There must be four or five dogs in the pack, I thought; and surely now they are driving down the old runway that crosses the brook at my meadow.

I kept my eye upon the bend in the brook and just beyond the big swamp maple, when there in the open road stood the fox.

He did not stand; he only seemed to, so suddenly and unannounced had he arrived. Not an instant had he to spare. The dogs were smashing through the briars behind him. Leaping into the middle of the road, he flew past me straight up the street, over the ridge, and out of sight.

I turned to see the burst of the pack into the road, when flash! a yellow streak, a rush of feet, a popping of dew-laid dust in the road, and back was the fox, almost into the jaws of the hounds, as he shot into the tangle of wild grapevines around which the panting pack was even then turning!

With a rush that carried them headlong past the grapevines, the dogs struck the warm trail in the road and went up over the hill in a whirlwind of dust and howls.

They were gone. The hunt was over for that day. Somewhere beyond the end of the doubled trail the pack broke up and scattered through the woods, hitting a stale lead here and there, but not one of them, so long as I waited, coming back upon the right track to the grapevines, through whose thick door the hard-pressed fox had so narrowly won his way.

CHAPTER III

IN THE TOADFISH'S SHOE

WAS winding up my summer vacation with a little fishing party all by myself, on a wharf whose piles stood deep in the swirling waters from Buzzards Bay. My heavy-leaded line hummed taut in the swift current; my legs hung limp above the water; my back rested comfortably against a great timber that was warm in the September sun. Exciting? Of course not. Fishing is fishing—any kind of fishing is fishing to me. But the kind I am most used to, and the kind I like best, is from the edge of a wharf, where my feet dangle over, where my "throw-out" line hums taut over my finger, in a tide that runs swift and deep and dark below me.

For what may you not catch in such dark waters? And when there are no "bites," you can sit and wait; and I think that sitting and waiting with my back against a big warm timber is just as much fun now as it used to be when I was a boy.

But after all it is fish that you want when you go fishing; and it is exciting, moreover, just to sit as I was sitting on the wharf, with all the nerves of your body concentrated in the tip of your right forefinger, under the pressure of your line. For how do you know but that the next instant you may get a bite? And how do you know what the fish may be?

When you whip a trout stream for trout—why, you expect trout; when you troll a pond for pickerel, you expect pickerel; but when you sit on a wharf with your line far out in big, deep waters—why, you can expect almost anything—except shoes!

Shoes? Yes, old shoes!

As I sat there on the wharf of Buzzards Bay, there was suddenly a sharp tug at my line. A short quick snap, and I hooked him, and began quickly hauling him in.

How heavily he came! How dead and stupid! Even a flounder or a cod would show more fight than this; and very naturally, for on the end of my line hung an old shoe!

"Well," I thought, "I have fished for soles, and down on the Savannah I have fished for 'gators, but I never fished for shoes before"; and taking hold of my big fish (for it must have been a No. 12 shoe), I was about to feel for the hook when I heard a strange grunting noise inside, and nearly tumbled overboard at sight of two big eyes and a monstrous head filling the whole inside of the shoe!

"In the name of Davy Jones!" I yelled, flinging line and shoe and *thing* (whatever it might be) far behind me, "I've caught the Old Man of the Sea with his shoe on!" And, scrambling to my feet, I hurried across the wharf to see if it really were a fish that now lay flapping close beside the shoe.

It was really a fish; but it was also a hobgoblin, nightmare, and ooze-croaker!—if you know what that is!

I had never seen a live toadfish before, and it is small wonder that I sighed with relief to see that he had unhooked himself; for he looked not only uncanny, but also dangerous! He was slimy all over, with a tremendous head and a more tremendous mouth (if that could be), with jaws studded on the inside with rows of sharp teeth, and fringed on the outside with folds of loose skin and tentacles. Great glaring eyes stared at me, with ragged bits of skin hanging in a ring about them.

Ugly? Oh, worse than ugly? Two thirds of the monster was head; the rest, a weak, shapeless, slimy something with fins and tail, giving the creature the appearance of one whose brain had grown at the expense of the rest of his body, making him only a kind of living head.

I looked at him. He looked at me, and croaked.

"I don't understand you," said I, and he croaked again. "But you are alive," said I; "and God made you, and therefore you ought not to look so ugly to me," and he flapped in the burning sun and croaked again.

Stooping quickly, I seized him, crowded him back into the old shoe, and dipped him under water. He gasped with new life and croaked again.

"Now," said I, "I begin to understand you. That croak means that you are glad to taste salt water again"; and he croaked again, and I dipped him in again.

Then I looked him over thoughtfully. He was about fifteen inches long, brown in color, and coarsely marbled with a darker hue, which ran along the fins in irregular wavy lines.

"You are odd, certainly, and peculiar, and altogether homely," said I; "but really you are not very ugly. Ugly? No, you are *not* ugly. How could anybody be ugly with a countenance so wise and learned?—so thoughtful and meditative?" And the toadfish croaked and croaked again. And I dipped

"HERE I FOUND HIM KEEPING HOUSE"

him in again, and understood him better, and liked him better all the time.

Then I took him in his shoe to the edge of the wharf.

"I am glad to have made your acquaintance, sir," said I. "If I come this way next summer, I shall look you up; for I want to know more about you. Good-by." And I heard him croak "Good-by," as he and his shoe went sailing out and dropped with a splash into the deep dark water of the Bay.

I meant what I said, and the next summer, along the shores of the Bay I hunted him up. He was not in an old shoe this time, but under certain rather large stones that lay just below ebb-tide mark, so that they were usually, though not always, covered with water. Here I found him keeping house; and as I was about to keep house myself, my heart really warmed to him.

I was understanding him more and more, and so I was liking him better and better. Ugly? Wait until I tell you what the dear fellow was doing.

He was keeping house, and he was keeping it all alone! Now listen, for this is what I learned that summer about the strange habits of Mrs. Toadfish, and the handsome behavior of her husband.

It is along in June that the toadfish of our New England bays begin to look round for their summer homes. As far as we now know, it is the female who makes the choice and leaves her future mate to find her and her home. A rock is usually chosen, always in shallow water, and sometimes so far up on the shore that at low tide it is left high and almost dry. The rock may vary in size from one as small as your hat up to the very largest.

Having selected the place for her nest, she digs a pathway down under the rock, and from beneath scoops out a hollow quite large enough to swim round in. This completes the nest, or more properly burrow, in which her little toadfish babies are to be reared.

She now begins to lay the eggs, but not in the sand, as one would suppose; she deliberately pastes them on the under surface of the rock. Just how she does this no one knows.

The eggs are covered with a clear, sticky paste which hardens in contact with water, and is the means by which the mother sticks them fast to the rock. This she must do while swimming on her back, fastening one egg at a time, each close beside its neighbor in regular order, till all the cleared surface of the rock is covered with hundreds of beautiful amber eggs, like drops of pure, clear honey.

The eggs are about the size of buckshot; and, curiously enough, when they hatch, the young come out with their heads all turned in the same direction. Does the mother know which is the head end of the egg? Or has some strange power drawn them around? Or do they turn themselves for some reason?

It will be noticed, in lifting up the rocks, that the heads of the fish are always turned toward the entrance to their nest, through which the light and fresh water come; and it is quite easy to see that these two important things have much to do with the direction in which the little fish are turned.

After Mrs. Fish has finished laying her eggs, her maternal cares are over. She leaves both eggs and cares to the keeping of Mr. Fish, swims off, and crawls into a tin can—or old shoe!—to meditate in sober satisfaction for the rest of the summer.

So it was *she* that I caught, and not the gallant Mr. Toadfish at all! I am glad of it. I have a deal of sympathy and down-right admiration for Mr. Fish. He behaves most handsomely.

However, Mrs. Fish is very wise, and could not leave her treasures in better keeping. If ever there was a faithful parent, it is a Father Toadfish. For three weeks he guards the eggs before they hatch out, and then they are only half hatched; for it has taken the little fish all this time to get out on the top side of the eggs, to which they are still attached by their middles, so that they can move only their heads and tails.

They continue to wiggle in this fashion for some weeks, until the yolk of the egg is absorbed, and they have grown to be nearly half an inch long. They are then free from the rock and swim off, looking as much like their parents as children can, and every bit as ugly.

Ugly? Did I say ugly? Is a baby ever ugly to its mother? Or a baby toadfish to its father? No. You cannot love a baby and at the same time see it ugly. You cannot love the out of doors with all your *mind* as well as with all your heart, and ever see it ugly.

All this time the father has been guarding the little toadfish; and if, during the whole period, he goes out to get a meal, I have not been able to find when it is, for I always find him at home, minding the babies.

The toadfish lives entirely unmolested by enemies, so far as I can learn; and his appearance easily explains the reason of it. I know of nothing that would willingly enter a croaking, snapping, slimy toadfish's nest to eat him; and it takes some courage to put one's hand into his dark hole and pull him out.

His principal diet seems to be shrimp, worms and all kinds of small fish. Yet he may be said to have no principal diet; for, no matter what you are fishing for, or what kind of bait you are using, if there is a toadfish in the vicinity you are sure to catch him. If fishing along a wharf in September, you may catch the fish, and an old shoe along with him—with *her*, perhaps I should say.

And if you do, please notice how wise and thoughtful the face, how beautifully marbled the skin, how courageous the big strong jaw!

Ugly? Not if you will put yourself in the toadfish's shoe.

CHAPTER IV

A CHAPTER OF THINGS TO SEE THIS FALL

I

YOU ought to see the sky—every day. You ought to see, as often as possible, the breaking of dawn, the sunset, the moonrise, and the stars. Go up to your roof, if you live in the city, or out into the middle of the Park, or take a street-car ride into the edge of the country—just to see the moon come up over the woods or over a rounded hill against the sky.

II

You ought to see the light of the October moon, as it falls through a roof of leafless limbs in some silent piece of woods. You have seen the woods by daylight; you have seen the moon from many places; but to be in the middle of the moonlit woods after the silence of the October frost has fallen is to have one of the most beautiful experiences possible out of doors.

III

You ought to see a wooded hillside in the glorious colors of the fall—the glowing hickories, the deep flaming oaks, the cool, dark pines, the blazing gums and sumacs! Take some single, particular woodland scene and look at it until you can see it in memory forever.

IV

You ought to see the spiders in their airships, sailing over the autumn meadows. Take an Indian Summer day, lazy, hazy, sunny, and lie down on your back in some small meadow where

woods or old rail fences hedge it around. Lie so that you do not face the sun. The sleepy air is heavy with balm and barely moves. Soon shimmering, billowing, through the light, a silky skein of cobweb will come floating over. Look sharply, and you will see the little aëronaut swinging in his basket at the bottom of the balloon, sailing, sailing—

Away in the air air—
Far are the shores of Anywhere,
Over the woods and the heather.

V

You ought to see (only *see*, mind you,) on one of these autumn nights, when you have *not* on your party clothes—you ought to see a "wood pussy." A wood pussy is not a house pussy; a wood pussy is a wood pussy; that is to say, a wood pussy is a—*skunk*! Yes, you ought to see a skunk walking calmly along a moonlit path and not caring a fig for you. You will perhaps never meet a wild buffalo or a grizzly bear or a jaguar in the woods nearest your house; but you may meet a wild skunk there, and have the biggest adventure of your life. Yes, you ought to see a skunk some night, just for the thrill of meeting a wild creature that won't get out of your way.

VI

You ought to see the witch-hazel bush in blossom late in November. It is the only bush or tree in the woods that is in full bloom after the first snow may have fallen. Many persons who live within a few minutes' walk of the woods where it grows have never seen it. But then, many persons who live with the sky right over their heads, with the dawn breaking right into their bedroom windows, have never seen the sky or the dawn to think about them, and wonder at them! There are many persons who have never seen anything at all that is worth seeing. The witch-hazel bush, all yellow with its strange blossoms in November, is worth seeing, worth taking a great deal of trouble to see.

There is a little flower in southern New Jersey called pyxie,

or flowering moss, a very rare and hidden little thing; and I know an old botanist who traveled five hundred miles just to have the joy of seeing that little flower growing in the sandy swamp along Silver Run. If you have never seen the witch-hazel in bloom, it will pay you to travel five hundred and five miles to see it. But you won't need to go so far,—unless you live beyond the prairies,—for the witch-hazel grows from Nova Scotia to Florida and west to Minnesota and Alabama.

There is one flower that, according to Mr. John Muir (and he surely knows!), it will pay one to travel away up into the highest Sierra to see. It is the fragrant Washington lily, "the finest of all the Sierra lilies," he says. "Its bulbs are buried in shaggy chaparral tangles, I suppose for safety from pawing bears; and its magnificent panicles sway and rock over the top of the rough snow-pressed bushes, while big, bold, blunt-nosed bees drone and mumble in its polleny bells. A lovely flower worth going hungry and footsore endless miles to see. The whole world seems richer now that I have found this plant in so noble a landscape."

'A WILD CREATURE THAT WON'T GET OUT OF YOUR WAY'

And so it seemed to the old botanist who came five hundred miles to find the tiny pyxie in the sandy swamps of southern New Jersey. So it will seem to you—the whole world will not only *seem* richer, but will *be* richer for you—when you have found the witch-hazel bush all covered with summer's gold in the bleak woods of November.

VII

You ought to see a big pile of golden pumpkins in some farmhouse shed or beside the great barn door. You ought to see a field of corn in the shock; hay in a barn mow; the jars of

fruit, the potatoes, apples, and great chunks of wood in the farmhouse cellar. You ought to see how a farmer gets ready for the winter—the comfort, the plenty, the sufficiency of it all!

VIII

You ought to see how the muskrats, too, get ready for the winter, and the bees and the flowers and the trees and the frogs—everything. Winter is coming. The cold will kill—if it has a chance. But see how it has no chance. How is it that the bees will buzz, the flowers open, the birds sing, the frogs croak again next spring as if there had been no freezing, killing weather? Go out and see why for yourselves.

IX

You ought to see the tiny seed "birds" from the gray birches, scattering on the autumn winds; the thistledown, too; and a dozen other of the winged, and plumed, and ballooned, seeds that sail on the wings of the winds. You should see the burdock burs in the cows' tails when they come home from the pasture, and the stick-tights and beggar-needles in your own coat-tails when you come home from the pastures. And seeing that, you should *think*—for that is what real seeing means. Think what? Why, that you are just as good as a cow's tail to scatter Nature's seeds for her, and not a bit better, as she sees you.

X

You ought to see the migrating birds as they begin to flock on the telegraph wires, in the chimneys, and among the reeds of the river. You ought to see the swallows, blackbirds, robins,

and bluebirds, as they flock together for the long southern flight. There are days in late September and in
early October when the very air seems to be half of
birds, especially toward nightfall, if the sun sets
full and clear: birds going over; birds diving and
darting about you; birds along the rails and
ridge-poles; birds in the grass under
your feet—birds everywhere. You
should be out among them where
you can see them. And especially
you should see—
without fail, this
autumn and every autumn—
the wedge of wild geese cleaving
the dull gray sky in their thrilling journey
down from the far-off frozen North.

CHAPTER V
WHIPPED BY EAGLES

S you head into Maurice River Cove from Delaware Bay by boat, the great eagle's nest of Garren's Neck Swamp soon looms into view. It is a famous nest, and an ancient nest; for it has a place in the chart of every boat that sails up the river, and has had for I don't know how many years. From the river side of the long swamp the nest is in sight the year round, but from the land side, and from the house where we lived, the nest could be seen only after the leaves of the swamp had fallen. Then all winter long we could see it towering over the swamp; and often, in the distance, we could see the eagles coming and going or soaring in mighty circles high up in the air above it.

That nest had a strange attraction for me. It was the home of eagles, the monarchs of this wide land of swamp and marsh and river.

Between me and the great nest lay a gloomy gum swamp, wet and wild, untouched by the axe and untraveled, except in winter by the coon-hunters. The swamp began just across the road that ran in front of the house; and often at night I would hear the scream of a wild cat in the dark hollows; and once I heard the *pat, pat* of its feet as it went leaping along the road.

Then beyond the swamp and the nest stretched a vast wild marsh-land, where the reeds grew, and the tides came in, and the mud-hens lived. And beyond that flowed the river, and beyond the river lay another marsh, and beyond the marsh another swamp. And over all this vast wild world towered the nest of the eagles, like some ancient castle; and over it all—swamp and marsh and river—ruled the eagles, as bold and free as the mighty barons of old.

Is it any wonder that I often found myself gazing away at that nest on the horizon and longing for wings?—for wings with which to soar above the swamp and the bay and the marsh and the river, to circle about and about that lofty eyrie, as wild as the eagles and as free? Is it any wonder that I determined some day to stand up in that nest, wings or no wings, while the eagles should scream about me, and away below me should stretch river and marsh and swamp?

To stand up in that nest, to yell and wave my arms with the eagles wheeling and screaming over me, became the very peak of my boy ambitions.

And I did it. I actually had the eggs of those eagles in my hands. I got into the nest; but I am glad even now that I got out of the nest and reached the ground.

It must have been in the spring of my fourteenth year when, at last, I found myself beneath the eagle tree. It was a stark old white oak, almost limbless, and standing out alone on the marsh some distance from the swamp. The eagle's nest capped its very top.

The nest, I knew, must be big; but not until I had climbed

up close under it did I realize that it was the size of a small haystack. There was certainly half a cord of wood in it. I think that it must originally have been built by fish hawks.

Holding to the forking top upon which the nest was placed, I reached out, but could not touch the edge from any side.

I had come determined to get up into it, however, at any hazard; and so I set to work. I never thought of how I was to get down; nor had I dreamed, either, of fearing the eagles. A bald eagle is a bully. I would as soon have thought of fearing our hissing old gander at home.

As I could not get out to the edge of the nest and scale the walls, the only possible way up, apparently, was through the nest. The sticks here in the bottom were old and quite rotten. Digging was easy, and I soon had a good beginning.

The structure was somewhat cone-shaped, the smaller end down. It had grown in circumference as it grew in years and in height, probably because at the bottom the building materials had decayed and gradually fallen away, until now there was a decided outward slant from bottom to top. It had grown lopsided, too, there being a big bulge on one side of the nest near the middle.

The smallness of the bottom at first helped me; there was less of the stuff to be pulled out. I easily broke away the dead timbers and pushed aside the tougher sticks. I intended to cut a channel clear to the top and go up through the nest. Already my head and shoulders were well into it.

Now the work became more difficult. The sticks were newer, some of them being of seasoned oak and hickory, which the birds had taken from cord-wood piles.

I had cut my channel up the side of the nest nearly halfway

when I came to a forked branch that I could neither break off nor push aside. I soon found that it was not loose, but that it belonged to the oak tree itself. It ran out through the nest horizontally, extending a little more than a foot beyond the rough walls.

Backing down, I saw that this fork was the support of the bulge that had given the nest its lopsided appearance. A few large timbers had been rested across it, small loose pieces had gradually lodged upon these, and thus in time brought about the big bulge.

I pushed off this loose stuff and the few heavy timbers and found that the fork would bear my weight. It now projected a little way from the walls of the nest. I got a firm hold on the forks out at their ends, swung clear, and drew myself up between them. After a lively scramble, I got carefully to my feet, and, clutching the sticks protruding from the side, stood up, with my eyes almost on a level with the rim of the great nest. This was better than cutting a channel, certainly—at least for the ascent, and I was not then thinking of the descent.

I looked over the protruding sticks of the rim. I caught a glimpse of large dull white eggs!

Eggs of shining gold could not have so fascinated me. There were thousands of persons who could have gold eggs if they cared. But eagles' eggs! Money could not buy such a sight as this.

I was more than ever eager now to get into the nest. Working my fingers among the sticks of the rim for a firm grip, I stuck my toes into the rough wall and began to climb. At some considerable hazard and at the cost of many rents in my clothing, I wriggled up over the edge and into the hollow of the nest where the coveted eggs lay.

The eagles were wheeling and screaming overhead. The weird *cac, cac, cac* of the male came down from far above me; while the female, circling closer, would swoop and shrill her menacing, maniacal half-laugh almost in my ears.

Their wild cries thrilled me, and their mighty wings, wheeling so close around me, seemed to catch me in their majestic sweep and almost to carry me in swift, swinging circles through the empty air. An ecstasy of excitement overcame me. I felt no body, no weight of anything. I lost my head completely, and, seizing the eggs, rose to my feet and stood upright in the nest.

The eagles swept nearer. I could feel the wind from their wings. I could see the rolling of their gleaming eyes, and the glint of the sun on their snow-white necks. And as they dipped and turned and careened over me, I came perilously near trying to fly myself.

What a scene lay under me and rolled wide and free to the very edge of the world! The level marsh, the blue, hazy bay, the far-off, unblurred horizon beyond the bending hill of the sea! The wild, free wind from the bay blew in upon my face, the old tree trembled and rocked beneath me, the screaming eagles wove a mazy spell of double circles about me, till I screamed back at them in wild delight.

The sound of my voice seemed to infuriate the birds. The male turned suddenly in his round and swooped directly at me. The movement was instantly understood by his mate, who, thus emboldened, cut under him and hurled herself downward, passing with a vicious grab at my face. I dodged, or she would have hit me.

For the moment I had forgotten where I stood; and, in dodging the eagle, I almost stepped over the edge of the nest.

I caught my balance and dropped quickly to my knees, completely unnerved.

Fear like a panic took instant hold on me. Only one desire possessed me—to get down. I crept to the edge and looked over. The sight made me dizzy. Sixty feet of almost empty air! Far down, a few small limbs intervened between me and the ground. But there was nothing by which to descend.

I was dismayed; and my expression, my posture—something, betrayed my confusion to the eagles. They immediately lost all dread of me. While I was looking over, one of them struck me a stinging blow on the head, knocking my cap off into the air.

That started me. I must climb down or be knocked over. If only I had continued with my channel to the top! If only that forked branch by which I ascended were within reach! But how could I back over the flaring rim to my whole length and swing my body under against the inward-slanting nest until my feet could touch the fork? But if I ever got down, that was what I must do; for the eagles gave me no chance to cut a channel now.

Laying the eggs back for the time in the hollow, I began tearing away the rim of the nest in order to clear a place over which to back down.

I was momentarily in danger of being hurled off by the birds; for I could not watch them and work, too. And they were growing bolder with every dash. One of them, driving fearfully from behind, flattened me out on the nest. Had the blow been delivered from the front, I should have been knocked headlong to the ground.

I was afraid to delay longer. A good-sized breach was

opened in the rim of the nest by this time. And now, if the sticks would not pull out, I might let myself over and reach the fork. Once my feet touched that, I could manage the rest, I knew.

Digging my hands deep into the nest for a firm hold, I began cautiously to back over the rough, stubby rim, reaching with my feet toward the fork.

The eagles seemed to appreciate the opportunity my awkward position offered them. I could not have arranged myself more conveniently to their minds, I am sure. And they made the most of it. I can laugh now; but the memory of it can still make me shiver, too.

I had wriggled over just so that I could bend my body at the waist and bring my legs against the nest when a sharp stub caught in my clothes and held me. I could get neither up nor down. My handhold was of the most precarious kind, and I dared not let go for a moment to get off the snag.

I tried to back out and push off from it, but it seemed to come out with me. It must be broken; and pulling myself up, I dropped with all the force I could put into my body. That loosened, but did not break it. Suddenly, while I was resting between the efforts, the thing gave way.

I was wholly unprepared. All my weight was instantly thrown upon my hands. The jagged sticks cut into my wrists, my grip was pried off, and I fell.

Once, twice, the stubs in the wall of the nest caught and partly stopped me, then broke. I clutched frantically at them, but could not hold. Then, almost before I realized that I was falling, I hung suspended between two limbs—the forks of the white oak branch in the side of the nest.

I had been directly above it when the stub broke, and had fallen through it; and the two branches had caught me right under both of my arms.

For a second I was too dazed to think. Then a swish of wings, a hard blow on the neck, and a shooting pain made my position clear. I was not down yet nor out of danger. The angry birds still had me in reach.

Hanging with one arm, I twisted round until the other arm was free, then seized the branches and swung under, but not before the eagles had given me another raking dab.

Here beneath the branches, close up to the bottom of the nest, I was quite out of the reach of the birds; and through the channel I had cut in my ascent, I climbed quickly down into the tree.

It was now a mere matter of sliding to the ground. But I was so battered and faint that I nearly tumbled. I was a sorry-looking boy—my clothing torn, my hands bleeding, my head and neck clawed in a dozen places.

But what did I do with the eagles' eggs? Why, I allowed the old eagles to hatch them. What else could I do? or what better?

CHAPTER VI

THANKSGIVING AT GRANDFATHER'S FARM

THANKSGIVING at Grandfather's farm was more than a holiday. It was a great date on the calendar, for it divided the year in halves as no other single day of the three hundred and sixty-five did. It marked the end of the outdoors, and the beginning of the indoors—the day when everybody came home; when along with them into the house came all the outdoors, too, as if the whole farm were brought in to toast its toes before the great hearth fire!

For the hearth fire was big enough and cheery enough. And so was the farmhouse—that is, if you added the big barn and the crib-house and the wagon-house and the dog-house and the hen-house and the "spring-house!"

Oh, there was plenty of room inside for everybody and for everything! And there needed to be; for did not everybody come home to Grandfather's for Thanksgiving? And did not everything that anybody could need for the winter, grow on Grandfather's farm?

And it all had to be brought in by Thanksgiving Day—everything brought in, everything housed and stored and battened down tight. The preparations began along in late October, continuing with more speed as the days shortened and darkened and hurried us into November. And they continued with still more speed as the gray lowering clouds thickened in the sky, and the wind began to whistle through the oak grove. Then, with the first real cold snap, the first swift flurry of snow, how the husking and the stacking and the chopping went on!

Thanksgiving must find us ready for winter indoors and out.

The hay-mows were full to the beams where the swallows built; the north and west sides of the barnyard were flanked with a deep wind-break of corn-fodder that ran on down the old worm-fence each side of the lane in yellow zigzag walls; the big wooden pump under the turn-o'-lane tree by the barn was bundled up and buttoned to the tip of its dripping nose; the bees by the currant bushes were doubled-hived, the strawberries covered with hay, the wood all split and piled, the cellar windows packed, and the storm-doors put on.

The very cows had put on an extra coat, and turned their collars up about their ears; the turkeys had changed their roost from the ridge-pole of the corn-crib to the pearmain tree on the sunny side of the wagon-house; the squirrels had finished their

"THE LANTERN FLICKERS, THE MILK FOAMS, THE STORIES FLOW"

bulky nests in the oaks; the muskrats of the lower pasture had completed their lodges; the whole farm—house, barn, fields, and wood-lot—had shuffled into its greatcoat and muffler and settled comfortably down for the winter.

The old farmhouse was an invitation to winter. It looked its joy at the prospect of the coming cold. Low, weather-worn, mossy-shingled, secluded in its wayward garden of box and bleeding-hearts, sheltered by its tall pines, grape-vined, hop-vined, clung to by creeper and honeysuckle, it stood where the roads divided, halfway between everywhere, unpainted, unpretentious, as much a part of the landscape as the muskrat-lodge, and, like the lodge, roomy, warm, and hospitable.

Round at the back, under the wide, open shed, a door led into the kitchen; another led into the living-room; another, into the store-room; and two big, slanting double-doors, scoured and slippery with four generations of sliders, covered the cavernous way into the cellar. But they let the smell of apples up, as the garret door let the smell of sage and thyme come down; while from the door of the store-room, mingling with the odor of apples and herbs, filling the whole house and all my early memories, came the smell of broom-corn, came the sound of Grandfather's loom.

For Grandfather in the winter made brooms—the best brooms, I think, that ever were made. The tall broom-corn was grown on the farm in the summer, ripened and cut and seeded, and then, as soon as winter set in, was loomed and wired and sewed into brooms.

But the cured and seeded broom-corn was not the main thing, after all, that was brought in for the winter. Behind the stove in the kitchen, stood the sweet-potato box (a sweet potato, you know, must be kept dry and warm). An ample, ten-barrel box it was, fresh-papered like the walls, full of Jersey sweets that *were* sweet—long, golden, syrupy potatoes, such as grow only in the warm sandy soil of southern New Jersey.

Against that big box in Grandmother's kitchen stood the sea-chest, fresh with the same kitchen paper and piled with wood. There was another such chest in the living-room near the old fireplace, and still another in Grandfather's work-room behind the "template" stove.

But wood and warmth and sweet smells were not all. There was music also, the music of life, of young life and of old life—grandparents, grandchildren (about twenty-eight of the latter). There were seven of us alone—a girl at each end of the seven and one in the middle. Thanksgiving always found us all at Grandfather's and brimming full of thanks.

That, of course, was long, long ago. Things are different nowadays. There are as many grandfathers, I suppose, as ever; but they don't make brooms in the winter and live on farms.

They live in flats. The old farm with its open acres has become a city street; the generous old farmhouse has become a speaking-tube, kitchenette, and bath—all the "modern conveniences"; the cows have evaporated into convenient cans of condensed "milk"; the ten-barrel box of potatoes has changed into a convenient ten-pound bag, the wood-pile into a convenient five-cent bundle of blocks tied up with a tarred string, the fireplace into a convenient gas log, the seven children into one or none, or into a little bull-terrier pup.

But is it so? No, it is not so—not so of a million homes. For there is many an old-fashioned farmhouse still in the country, and many a new-fashioned city house where there are more human children than little bull-terrier pups.

And it is not so in my home, which is neither a real farm nor yet a city home. For here are some small boys who live very much as I did when I was a boy. No, they are not farmer's boys; for I am not a farmer, but only a "commuter"—if you know what that is. I go into a great city for my work; and when the day's work is done, I turn homeward here to Mullein Hill—far out in the country. And when the dark November nights come, I hang the lantern high in the stable, as my father used to do, while four shining faces gather round, as four small boys seat themselves on upturned buckets behind the cow. The lantern flickers, the milk foams, the stories flow—"Bucksy" stories of the noble red-man; and stories of the heroes of old; and marvelous stories of that greatest hero of all—their father, far away yonder when he was a boy, when there were so many interesting things to do on Grandfather's farm just before Thanksgiving Day.

CHAPTER VII

A CHAPTER OF THINGS
TO DO THIS FALL

I

OU ought to go out into the fields and woods as many as six times this fall, even though you have to take a long street-car ride to get out of the city. Let me give you just six bits of sound advice about going afield:—

First, go often to the same place, so that you can travel over and over the same ground and become very familiar with it. The first trip you will not see much but woods and fields. But after that, each succeeding walk will show you *particular* things—this dead tree with the flicker's hole, that old rail-pile with its rabbit-hole—until, by and by, you will know every turn and dip, every pile of stones, every hole and nest; and you will find a thousand things that on the first trip you didn't dream were there.

Secondly, when you go into the woods, go *expecting* to see something in particular—always looking for some particular nest, bird, beast, or plant. You may not find that particular thing, but your eyes will be sharpened by your expectation and purpose, and you will be pretty sure therefore to see something. At worst you will come back with a disappointment, and that is better than coming back without a thing!

Thirdly, go off when you can alone. Don't be selfish, unsociable, offish—by no means that. But you must learn to use your own eyes and ears, think your own thoughts, make your own discoveries, and follow the hints and hopes that you alone can have. Go with the school class for a picnic, but for woodcraft go alone.

Fourthly, learn first of all in the woods to be as silent as an Indian and as patient as a granite rock. Practice standing still when the mosquitoes sing, and fixing your mind on the hole under the stump instead of the hole the mosquito is boring between your eyes.

Fifthly, go out in every variety of weather, and at night, as well as during the day. There are three scenes to every day—morning, noon, and early evening—when the very actors themselves are changed. To one who has never been in the fields at daybreak, the world is so new, so fresh and strange, as to seem like a different planet. And then the evening—the hour of dusk and the deeper, darker night! Go once this autumn into the woods at night.

And lastly, don't go into the woods as if they were a kind

of Noah's Ark; for you cannot enter the door and find all the animals standing in a row. You will go a great many times before seeing them all. Don't be disappointed if they are not so plentiful there as they are in your books. Nature books are like menageries—the animals are caught and caged for you. The woods are better than books and just as full of things, as soon as you learn to take a hint, to read the signs, to put two and two together and get—four—four paws—black paws, with a long black snout, a big ringed and bushy tail—a coon!

II

Whether you live in the heart of a great city or in the open country, you ought to begin this fall to learn the names and habits of the birds and beasts (snakes, lizards, turtles, toads!)

that live wild in your region. Even when all the summer birds have gone south for the winter, there will remain in your woods and fields crows, jays, juncos, tree sparrows, chickadees, kinglets, nuthatches, screech owls, barred owls,—perhaps even snowy owls,—quails, partridges, goldfinches, with now and then a flock of crossbills, snow buntings, and other northern visitors, and even a flicker, robin, and bluebird left over from the fall migrations. These are plenty to begin on; and yet, as they are so few, compared with the numbers of the summer, the beginner's work is thus all the easier in the autumn.

III

You should go out one of these frosty mornings for chestnuts, if they grow in your woods; or for "shagbarks," if you live in New England; for black walnuts, if you live in the Middle States; for pecan nuts, if you live in the Gulf States; for butternuts, if you live in the states of the Middle West; for—what kind of nuts can you not go for, if you live in California where they make everything grow! It matters little whether you go for paper-shelled English walnuts or for plate-armored pignuts so long as you *go*. It is the going that is worth while.

IV

You ought to go "cocooning" this fall—to sharpen your eyes. But do not go often; for once you begin to look for cocoons, you are in danger of seeing nothing else—except brown leaves. And how many brown leaves, that look like cocoons, there are! They tease you to vexation. But a day now and then "cocooning" will do you no harm; indeed, it will cultivate your habit of concentration and close seeing as will no other kind of hunting I know.

Bring home with you the big brown silky cocoons of cecropia—the largest cocoon you will find, lashed all along its length to its twig, and usually near the ground. Look on the black cherry, the barberry, sassafras, and roadside and garden trees for the harder, whiter cocoon of the promethea moth. This hangs by its tip, because the caterpillar has begun his house by using the leaf, spinning it into the cocoon as part of its walls, much as does the wretched "brown-tail." The gray cocoons, or rather nests, of this "brown-tail" moth you must bring home to burn, for they are one of our greatest pests. You will find them full of tiny caterpillars as you tear them open.

Bring home your collection and, with the help of such a book as "Moths and Butterflies" by Mary C. Dickerson, identify them and hang them up for their "coming out" in the spring.

V

If you live in the city, you ought to go up frequently to your roof and watch for the birds that fly over. If in one of our many cities near the water, you will have a chance that those in the country seldom have, of seeing the seabirds—the white herring gulls (the young gulls are brown, and look like a different species), as they pass over whistling plaintively, and others of the wild seafowl, that merely to hear and see in the smoky air of the city, is almost as refreshing as an ocean voyage. Then there are the parks and public gardens—never without their birds and, at the fall migrating time, often sheltering the very rarest of visitors.

VI

In order to give point and purpose to one of these autumn outings, you should take your basket, or botanizing can, and scour the woods and fields for autumn berries. No bunch of flowers in June could be lovelier than the bunch of autumn berries that you can gather from thicket and wayside to carry home. And then, in order to enjoy the trip all over again, read James Buckham's exquisite story, "A Quest for Fall Berries," in his book, "Where Town and Country Meet."

VII

Take your botany can on a trip toward the end of November and see how many blossoming flowers you can bring home from the woods. Wild flowers *after* Thanksgiving in any northern state? Make the search, on all the southern slopes and in all the sheltered corners and see for yourselves. When you get back, you will want to read Mr. Bradford Torrey's account of the flowers that he found blossoming out of doors in New England in the month of November. But who is Mr. Bradford Torrey? and where can you find this account of his November walk? You do not know? Well, then there is something more for you to do this fall.

VIII

While you are finding out who Mr. Torrey is and what he has written, you should also get acquainted with John Burroughs, Olive Thorne Miller, Thoreau, Frank Bolles, William Hamilton Gibson, C. C. Abbott, Edward Breck, Gilbert White, and—but these will do for *this* fall. Don't fail to read dear old Gilbert White's "Natural History of Selborne"; though perhaps we grown-ups like it better than you may this fall. If you don't understand Gilbert White, then read this year "The Life of a Scotch Naturalist" by Samuel Smiles, and Arabella Buckley's two books, "Life and Her Children," and "Winners in Life's Race."

IX

You ought to tie up a piece of suet for the birds; keep your cat in the house, except during the middle of the day, and—but I shall tell you no more. There is no end to the interesting things to do in your study of the out of doors and in your tramps afield this autumn.

CHAPTER VIII

THE MUSKRATS ARE BUILDING

E have had a week of almost unbroken rain, and the water is standing over the swampy meadow. It is a dreary stretch,—this wet, sedgy land in the cold twilight,—drearier than any part of the woods or the upland pastures. They are empty; but the meadow is flat and wet, it is naked and all unsheltered. And a November night is falling.

The darkness deepens. A raw wind is rising. At nine o'clock the moon swings round and full to the crest of the ridge, and pours softly over. I button my heavy ulster close, and in my rubber boots go down to the stream and follow it out to the middle of the meadow, where it meets the main ditch. There is a sharp turn here toward the swamp; and here at the bend, behind a clump of black alders, I sit quietly down and wait.

I have come out to the bend to watch the muskrats building; for that small mound up the ditch is not an old haycock, but a half-finished muskrat house.

As I wait, the moon climbs higher over the woods. The water

on the meadow shivers in the light. The wind bites through my heavy coat and drives me back, but not before I have seen one, two, three little creatures scaling the walls of the house with loads of mud-and-reed mortar. I am driven back by the cold, but not before I know that here in the desolate meadow is being rounded off a lodge, thick-walled and warm, and proof against the longest, bitterest of winters.

This is near the end of November. My fire-wood is in the cellar; I am about ready to put on the double-windows and the storm-doors. The muskrats are even now putting on theirs, for their house is all but finished. Winter is at hand: but we are prepared, the muskrats and I.

Throughout the summer the muskrats had no house, only their tunnels into the sides of the ditch, their roadways out into the grass, and their beds under the tussocks or among the roots of the old stumps. All those months the water was low in the ditch, and the beds among the tussocks were safe and dry enough.

Now the November rains have filled river and ditch, flooded the tunnels, and crept up into the beds under the tussocks. Even a muskrat will creep out of his bed when cold, wet water creeps in. What shall he do for shelter? He knows. And long before the rains begin, he picks out the place for a house. He does not want to leave his meadow, therefore the only thing to do is to build,—move from under the tussock out upon the top of the tussock; and here, in its deep, wiry grass, make a new bed high and dry above the rising water; and close this new bed in with walls that circle and dome, and defy the very winter.

Such a house will require a great deal of work to build. Why should not two or three muskrats combine—make the house

"TO-NIGHT THERE IS NO LOAFING ABOUT THE LODGE"

big enough to hold them all, save labor and warmth, too, and, withal, live sociably together? So they left, each one his single bed, and, joining efforts, started, about the middle of October, to build this winter house.

Slowly, night after night, the domed walls have been rising, although for several nights at a time I could see no apparent progress with the work. The builders were in no hurry. The cold was far off. But it is coming, and to-night it feels near and keen. And to-night there is no loafing about the lodge.

When this house is done, when the last hod of mud plaster has been laid on,—then the rains may descend and the floods come, but it will not fall. It is built upon a tussock; and a tussock—did you ever try to pull up a tussock?

Winter may descend, and boys and foxes may come—and they will come, but not before the walls are frozen. Then, let them come. The house will stand. It is boy-proof, almost; it is entirely rain-, cold-, and fox-proof. I have often seen where the fox has gone round and round the house in the snow, and where, at places, he has attempted to dig into the frozen mortar. But it was a foot thick, as hard as flint, and utterly impossible for his pick and shovel.

I said the floods, as well as the fox, may come. So they may, ordinarily; but along in March, when one comes as a freshet and rises to the dome of the house, then it fills the bed-chamber to the ceiling and drowns the dwellers out. I remember a freshet once in the end of February that flooded Lupton's Pond and drove the muskrats of the whole pond village to their ridgepoles, to the bushes, and to whatever wreckage the waters brought along.

"The best-laid schemes o' mice and men
Gang aft agley"

—and of muskrats, too.

But not very often do the muskrats' plans go thus agley. For muskrats and wood mice and birds and bees, and even the very trees of the forest, have a kind of natural foresight. They all look ahead, at the approach of autumn, and begin to provide against the coming cold. Yet, weather-wise as a muskrat may be, still he cannot know all that may happen; he cannot be ready for everything. And so, if now and then, he should prove foresight to be vain, he only shows that his plans and our plans, his life and our lives, are very much alike.

Usually, however, the muskrat's plans work out as he would have them. His foresight proves to be equal to all that the winter can bring. On the coldest winter days I shall look out over the bleak white waste to where his house shows, a tiny mound in the snow, and think of him safe and warm inside, as safe and warm as I am, in my house, here on the hilltop.

Indeed, I think the muskrat will be the warmer; for my big house here on Mullein Hill is sometimes cold. And the wind! If only I could drive the winter wind away from the corners of the house! But the house down in the meadow has no corners. It has walls, mud walls, so thick and round that the shrieking wind sweeps past unheard by the dwellers within; and all unheeded the cold creeps over and over the low thatch, to crawl back and stiffen upon the meadow.

The doors of this meadow house swing wide open throughout the winter; for they are in the bottom of the house, beneath the water, where only the muskrat can enter. Just outside the doors, down under the water and the roof of ice that covers all the flooded meadow, are fresh calamus roots, and iris and arum—food in abundance, no matter how long the winter lasts.

No, the winter has not yet come; but it is coming, for the muskrats are building. Let it come. Let the cold crawl stiff and gray across the meadow. Let the whirling snow curl like smoke about the pointed top of the little tepee down by the meadow ditch. Let the north wind do its worst. For what care the dwellers in that thick-walled lodge beneath the snow? Down under the water their doors are open; their roadways up the ditches as free as in the summer; and the stems of the sedges just as juicy and pink and tender.

The muskrats are building. The buds are leaving. Winter is coming. I must get out my own storm-windows and double-doors; for even now a fire is blazing cheerily on my wide, warm hearth.

CHAPTER IX

THE NORTH WIND DOTH BLOW

"The north wind doth blow,
And we shall have snow,
And what will poor Robin do then,
Poor thing?"

AND what will Muskrat do? and Chipmunk? and Whitefoot, the wood mouse? and Chickadee? and the whole world of poor things out of doors?

Never fear. Robin knows as well as you that the north wind doth blow, and is now far away on his journey to the South; Muskrat knows, too, and is building his warm winter lodge; Chipmunk has already made his bed deep down under the stone wall, where zero weather is unheard of; Whitefoot, the wood mouse, has stored his hollow poplar stub full of acorns, and, taking possession of Robin's deserted nest near by, has roofed it and lined it and turned it into a cosey, cold-proof house, while Chickadee, dear thing—has done nothing at all. Not so much as a bug or a single beetle's egg has he stored up for the winter. But he knows where there is a big piece of suet for him on a

certain lilac bush. And
he knows
where there
is a snug
l i t t l e
hole in a
certain elm
tree limb. The north

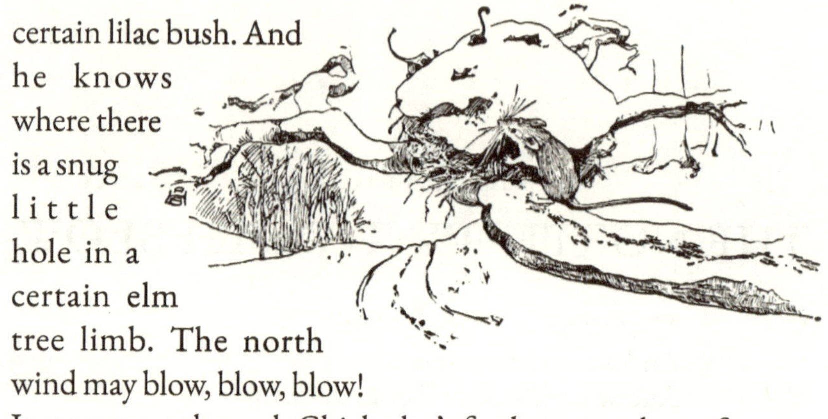

wind may blow, blow, blow!
It cannot get through Chickadee's feathers, nor daunt for one
moment his brave little heart.

The north wind sweeping the bare stubble fields and winding its shivering horn through the leafless trees does sometimes
pierce my warm coat and strike a chill into my heart. Then how
empty and cold seems the outdoor world! How deadly the touch
of the winter! How fearful the prospect of the coming cold!

Does Muskrat think so? Does Whitefoot? Does Chickadee?
Not at all, for they are ready.

The preparations for hard weather may be seen going on all
through the autumn, beginning as far back as the flocking of
the swallows late in July. Up to that time no one had thought
of a coming winter, it would seem; but, one day, there upon
the telegraph-wires were the swallows—the first sign that the
getting ready for winter has begun.

The great migratory movements of the birds are very mysterious; but they were in the beginning, I think, and are still, for
the most part, mere shifts to escape the cold. Yet not so much
to escape the cold itself do the birds migrate, as to find a land
of food. When the northland freezes, when river and lake are
sealed beneath the ice and the soil is made hard as flint, then the

food supplies for most of the birds are utterly cut off, causing them to move southward ahead of the cold, or starve.

There are, however, a few of the seed-eating birds, like the quail, and some of the insect-eaters, like the chickadee, who are so well provided for that they can stay and survive the winter. But the great majority of the birds, because they have no storehouse nor barn, must take wing and fly away from the lean and hungry cold.

And I am glad to see them go. The thrilling honk of the flying wild geese out of the November sky tells me that the hollow forests and closing bays of the vast desolate North are empty now, except for the few creatures that find food and shelter in the snow.

Here in my own small woods and marshes there is much getting ready, much comforting assurance that Nature is quite equal to herself, that winter is not approaching unawares. There will be great lack, no doubt, before there is plenty again; there will be suffering and death. But what with the building, the strange deep sleeping, and the harvesting, there will be also much comfortable, much joyous and sociable, living.

Long before the muskrats began to build, even before the swallows commenced to flock, my chipmunks started their winter stores. I don't know which began his work first, which kept harder at it, Chipmunk or the provident ant. The ant has a great reputation for thrift, and verses have been written about her. But Chipmunk is just as thrifty. So is the busy bee.

It is the thought of approaching winter that keeps the bee busy far beyond her summer needs. Much of her labor is entirely for the winter. By the first of August she has filled the brood chamber of the hive with honey—forty pounds of it, enough for the hatching bees and for the whole colony until the willows tassel again. But who knows what the winter may be? how cold and long drawn out into the coming May? So the harvesting is pushed with vigor on, until the frosts kill the last of the autumn asters—on, until fifty, a hundred, or even three hundred pounds of honey are sealed in the combs, and the colony is safe should the sun not shine again for a year and a day.

The last of the asters have long since gone; so have the witch-hazels. All is quiet about the hives. The bees have formed into their warm winter clusters upon the combs; and except "when come the calm, mild days," they will fly no more until March or April. I will half close their entrances—and so help them to put on their storm-doors.

The whole out of doors around me is like a great beehive, stored and sealed for the winter, its swarming life close-clustered, and safe and warm against the coming cold.

I stand along the edge of the hillside here and look down the length of its frozen slope. There is no sign of life. The brown leaves have drifted into the mouths of the woodchuck holes, as if every burrow were forsaken; sand and sticks have washed in, too, littering and choking the doorways. A stranger would find it hard to believe that all of my forty-six woodchucks are gently snoring at the bottoms of these old uninteresting holes. Yet here they are, and quite out of danger, sleeping the sleep of the furry, the fat, and the forgetful.

The woodchuck's manner of providing for winter is very

curious. Winter spreads far and fast, and Woodchuck, in order to keep ahead, out of danger, would need wings. But wings weren't given him. Must he perish then? Winter spreads far, but it does not go deep—down only about four feet; and Woodchuck, if he cannot escape overland, can, perhaps, escape *under*land. So down he goes *through* the winter, down into a mild and even temperature, *five feet away*—only five feet, but as far away from the snow and the cold as Bobolink among the reeds of the distant Orinoco.

Indeed, Woodchuck's is a farther journey and even more wonderful than Bobolink's; for these five feet carry him to the very gates of death. That he will return with Bobolink, that he will come up alive with the spring out of this dark way, is passing strange.

Muskrat built him a house, and under the spreading ice turned all the meadow into a well-stocked cellar. Beaver built him a dam, cut and anchored under water a plenty of green sticks near his lodge, so that he too would be under cover when the ice formed, with an abundance of tender bark at hand. Chipmunk spent half of his summer laying up food near his underground nest. But Woodchuck simply digged him a hole,—a grave,—then ate until no particle more of fat could be got within his baggy hide, then crawled into his bed to sleep until the dawn of spring!

This is his shift! This is the length to which he goes, because he has no wings, and because he cannot cut, cure, and store away, in the depths of the stony hillside, clover hay enough to last him through the winter. The beaver cans his fresh food in cold water; the chipmunk selects long-keeping things and buries them; but the woodchuck simply fattens himself, then buries himself, and sleeps—and lives!

> "The north wind doth blow,
> And we shall have snow,"

but what good reason is there for our being daunted at the prospect? Robin and all the others are well prepared. Even the wingless frog, who is also without fur or feathers or fat, even he has no fear at the sound of the cold winds. Nature provides for him, too, in her own motherly way. All he has to do is to dig into the mud at the bottom of the ditch and sleep—and sometimes freeze!

No matter. If the cold works down and freezes him into the mud, he never knows. He will thaw out as good as new; he will sing again for joy and love as soon as his heart warms up enough to beat. I have seen frogs frozen into the middle of solid lumps of ice. Drop the lump on the floor, and the frog would break out like a fragment of the ice itself. And this has happened more than once to the same frog without causing him the least ache or pain. He would gradually limber up, and croak, and look as wise as ever.

The north wind *may* blow, for it is by no means a cheerless prospect, this wood-and-meadow world of mine in the gray November light. The grass-blades are wilting, the old leaves are falling; but no square foot of greensward will the winter kill, nor a single tree perhaps in all my wood-lot. There will be little less of life next April because of this winter. The winter birds will suffer most, and a few may die.

Last February, I came upon two partridges in the snow, dead of hunger and cold. It was after an extremely long "severe spell"; but this was not the only cause. These two birds since fall had been feeding regularly in the dried fodder corn that stood shocked over the field. One day all the corn was carted away. The birds found their supply of food suddenly cut off, and, unused to foraging the fence-rows and tangles for wild seeds, they seem to have given up the struggle at once, although within easy reach of plenty.

Hardly a minute's flight away was a great thicket of dwarf sumac covered with berries. There were bayberries, rosehips, greenbrier, bittersweet, black alder, and checkerberries that they might have found. These berries would have been hard fare, doubtless, after an unstinted supply of sweet corn; but still they were plentiful and would have been sufficient had the birds made use of them.

The smaller birds that stay through the winter, like the tree sparrow and the junco, feed upon the weeds and grasses that ripen unmolested along the roadsides and in the waste places. A mixed flock of these small birds lived several days last winter upon the seeds of the ragweed in my mowing-field.

The weeds came up in the early fall after the field was sowed to clover and timothy. They threatened to choke out the grass. I looked at them and thought with dismay of how they would cover the field by another fall. After a time the snow came, a foot and a half of it, till only the tops of the seedy ragweeds showed above the level white. Then the juncos, goldfinches, and tree sparrows came; and there was a five-day shucking of ragweed seed on the crusty snow—five days of life and plenty for the birds.

Then I looked again, and thought that weeds and winters, which were made when the world was made—that even ragweeds and winters have a part in the beautiful divine scheme of things.

> "The north wind doth blow
> And we shall have snow"—

but the wild geese are going over; the wild mice have harvested their acorns; the bees have clustered; the woodchucks have gone to sleep; the muskrats have nearly finished their lodge; the sap in the big hickory tree by the side of the house has crept down out of reach of the fingers of the frost. And what has become of Robin, poor thing?

CHAPTER X
AN OUTDOOR LESSON

HAVE had many a person ask me, "What is the best way to learn about the out of doors?" and I always answer, "Don't try to learn *about* it, but first go out of the house and get into the out of doors. Then open both eyes, use both of your ears, and stand in one place stock still as long as you can; and you will soon know the out of doors itself, which is better than knowing about it."

"But," says my learner, "if I go out of the house, I don't get into the out of doors at all, but into a city street!"

Look there—in the middle of the street! What is it? An English sparrow? Yes, an English sparrow—six English sparrows. Are they not a part of the out of doors? And look up there, over your head—a strip of sky? Yes—is not a strip of blue sky a part of the out of doors?

Now let me tell you how I learned an outdoor lesson one night along a crowded city street.

It was a cold, wet night; and the thick, foggy twilight, settling down into the narrow streets, was full of smoke and smell and chill. A raw wind blew in from the sea and sent a shiver past every corner. The street lights blinked, the street mud glistened, the street noises clashed and rattled, and the street crowds poured up and down and bore me along with them.

I was homesick—homesick for the country. I longed to hear the sound of the wind in the pine trees; I longed to hear the single far-away bark of the dog on the neighboring farm, or the bang of a barndoor, or the clack of a guinea going to roost. It was half-past five, and thousands of clerks were pouring from the closing stores; but I was lonely, homesick for the quiet, the wideness, the trees and sky of the country.

Feeling thus, and seeing only the strange faces all about me, and the steep narrow walls of the street high above me, I drifted along, until suddenly I caught the sound of bird voices shrill and sharp through the din.

I stopped, but was instantly jostled out of the street, up against a grim iron fence, to find myself peering through the pickets into an ancient cemetery in the very heart of Boston.

As I looked, there loomed up in the fog and rain overhead the outlines of three or four gaunt trees, whose limbs were as thick with sparrows as they had ever been with leaves. A sparrow roost! Birds, ten thousand birds, gone to roost in the business section of a great city, with ten thousand human beings passing under them as they slept!

I got in behind a big waste-barrel by the iron fence and let the crowd surge past. It was such a sight as I had never seen. I had seen thousands of chimney swallows go to roost in the deserted chimneys of a great country house; I had many a time gone down at night to the great crow-roost in the pines at Cubby Hollow; but I had never stumbled upon a bird-roost on a crowded city street before!

The hurrying throng behind me thinned and straggled while

I waited, watching by the iron fence. The wind freshened, the mist thickened into fine rain that came slanting down through the half-lighted trees; the sleeping sparrows twittered and shifted uneasily on the limbs.

The streets were being deserted. It was going to be a wild night on the water, and a wild night in the swaying, creaking tops of these old elm trees. I shivered at the thought of the sparrows sleeping out in such a night as this, and turned away toward my own snug roost hardly two blocks away.

The night grew wilder. The wind rattled down our street past a hundred loose shutters; the rain slapped against the windows, and then stopped as a heavy gust curled over the line of roofs opposite. I thought of the sparrows. Had they been driven from the tossing limbs? Could they cling fast in such a wind, and could they sleep?

Going to the window I looked down into the street. Only the electric light at the corner showed through the blur of the storm. The street was empty.

I slipped into my coat and went out; not even a policeman was in sight. Only the whirling sheets of rain, only the wild sounds of the wind were with me. The lights flared, but only to fill the streets with fantastic shadows and to open up a yawning cavern in every deep, dark doorway.

Keeping in the lee of the shuttered buildings, I made my way to the sparrow roost. I shall never forget the sight! Not a sparrow had left his perch, but every bird had now turned, facing the wind—breasting the wind, I should say; for every head was under a wing, as near as I could make out, and every breast was toward the storm. Here, on the limbs, as close as beads on a string, they clung and rocked in the arms of the wind, every one with his feathers tight to his body, his tail lying out flat on the storm.

Now there is the outdoor lesson I learned, and that is how I learned it. And what was the lesson? Why, this: that you are not shut away from Nature even in the heart of a great city; that the out of doors lies very close about you, as you hurry down a crowded city street.

CHAPTER XI

LEAFING

O, you never went "leafing"—not unless you are simon-pure country-bred. You do not know what the word means. You cannot find it in the unabridged dictionary—not in the sense in which I am using it. But there are many good words we country people use that are not, perhaps, in the dictionary.

And what do I mean by "leafing"? Get down that bundle of meal sacks, hitch into the one-horse hay-rig, throw in the rakes, and come. We are going into the woods for pig-bedding, for leaves to keep the pigs dry and warm this winter!

You never went after leaves for the pigs? Perhaps you never even had a pig. But a pig is worth having, if only to see the comfort he takes in the big bed of dry leaves you give him in the sunny corner of his pen. And if leafing had no other reward, the thought of the snoozing, snoring pig buried to his winking snout in the bed, would give joy and zest enough to the labor.

But leafing, like every other humble labor, has its own rewards, not the least of them being the leaves themselves and the getting of them!

We jolt across the bumpy field, strike into the back wood-road, and turn off upon an old stumpy track over which cord

83

wood was carted years ago. Here in the hollow at the foot of a high wooded hill, the winds have whirled the oak and maple leaves into drifts almost knee-deep.

We are off the main road, far into the heart of the woods. We straddle stumps; bend down saplings; stop while the horse takes a bite of sweet birch; tack and tip and tumble and back through the tight squeezes between the trees; and finally, after a prodigious amount of whoa-ing and oh-ing and squealing and screeching, we land right side up and so headed that we can start the load out toward the open road.

You can yell all you want to when you go leafing; yell at every stump you hit; yell every time a limb knocks off your hat or catches you under the chin; yell when the horse stops suddenly to browse on the twigs and stands you meekly on your head in the bottom of the rig. You can screech and howl and yell like the wild Indian that you are, you can dive and wrestle in the piles of leaves and cut all the crazy capers you know; for this is a Saturday, these are the wild woods and the noisy leaves, and who is there looking on besides the mocking jays and the crows?

The leaves pile up. The wind blows keen among the tall, naked trees; the dull cloud hangs low above the ridge; and through the cold gray of the maple swamp below you, peers the face of Winter.

You start up the ridge with your rake and draw down another pile, thinking, as you work, of the pig. The thought is pleasing. The warm glow all over your body strikes into your heart. You rake away as if it were your own bed you were gathering—as really it is. He that rakes for his pig, rakes also for himself. A merciful man is merciful to his beast; and he that gathers leaves for his pig spreads a blanket of down over his own winter bed.

Is it to warm my feet on winter nights that I pull on my boots at ten o'clock and go my round at the barn? Yet it warms my feet through and through to look into the stalls and see the cow chewing her cud, and the horse cleaning up his supper hay, standing to his fetlocks in his golden bed of new rye-straw; and then, going to the pig's pen, to hear him snoring louder than the north wind, somewhere in the depths of his leaf-bed, far out of sight. It warms my heart, too!

So the leaves pile up. How good a thing it is to have a pig to work for! What zest and purpose it lends to one's raking and piling and storing! If I could get nothing else to spend myself on, I should surely get me a pig. Then, when I went to walk in the woods, I should be obliged, occasionally, to carry a rake and a bag with me—much better things to take into the woods than empty hands, and sure to scratch into light a number of objects that would never come within the range of opera-glass or gun or walking stick. To see things through a twenty-four-toothed rake is to see them very close, as through a microscope magnifying twenty-four diameters.

And so, as the leaves pile up, we keep a sharp lookout for what the rake uncovers—here, under a rotten stump, a hatful of acorns, probably gathered by the white-footed wood mouse. For the stump gives at the touch of the rake, and a light kick topples it down the hill, spilling out a big nest of feathers and three dainty little creatures that scurry into the leaf-piles like streaks of daylight. They are the white-footed wood mice, long-tailed, big-eared, and as clean and high-bred looking as greyhounds.

Combing down the steep hillside with our rakes, we dislodge a large stone, exposing a black patch of fibrous roots and leaf mould, in which something moves and disappears. Scooping up a double handful of the mould, we capture a little red-backed salamander.

This is not the "red" salamander that Mr. Burroughs tells us is "the author of that fine plaintive piping to be heard more or less frequently, according to the weather, in our summer and autumn woods." His "red" salamander is really a "dull orange, variegated with minute specks or spots," a species I have never found here in my New England woods.

Nor have I ever suspected my red-backed salamander of piping; though he may do it, as may the angleworms, for aught I am able to hear, so filled with whir of iron wheels are my dull ears. But listen! Something piping! Above the rustle of the leaves we also hear a "fine plaintive" sound—no, a shrill and ringing little racket, rather, about the bigness of a penny whistle.

Dropping the rake, we cautiously follow up the call—it seems to speak out of every tree trunk—and find the piper clinging to a twig, no salamander at all, but a tiny tree-frog, Pickering's hyla, his little bagpipe blown almost to bursting as he tries to rally the scattered summer by his tiny, mighty "skirl." Take him nose and toes, he is surely as much as an inch long, not very large to pipe against the north wind turned loose in the leafless woods.

We go back to our raking. Above us, among the stones of the slope, hang bunches of Christmas fern; around the foot of the trees we uncover trailing clusters of gray-green partridge vine, glowing with crimson berries; we rake up the prince's pine, pipsissewa, creeping jennie, and wintergreen red with ripe berries,—a whole bouquet of evergreens,—exquisite, fairy-like forms, that later shall gladden our Christmas table.

"BUT COME, BOYS, GET AFTER THOSE BAGS!"

But how they gladden and cheer the October woods! Summer dead? Hope all gone? Life vanished away? See here, under this big pine, a whole garden of arbutus, green and budded, almost ready to bloom! The snows shall come before their sweet eyes open; but open they will at the very first touch of spring. We will gather a few, and let them wake up in saucers of clean water in our sunny south windows.

Leaves for the pig, and arbutus for us! We make a clean sweep down the hillside, "jumping" a rabbit from its form, or bed, under a brush-pile; discovering where a partridge roosts in a low-spreading hemlock; coming upon a snail cemetery, in a hollow hickory stump; turning up a yellow-jacket's nest, built two-thirds underground; tracing the tunnel of a bobtailed mouse in its purposeless windings in the leaf mould; digging into a woodchuck's—

"But come, boys, get after those bags! It is leaves in the hay-rig that we want, not woodchucks at the bottom of woodchuck holes." Two small boys catch up a bag and hold it open, while the third boy stuffs in the crackling leaves. Then I come along with my big feet and pack the leaves in tight, and onto the rig goes the bulging thing!

Exciting? If you can't believe it exciting, hop up on the load and let us jog you home. Swish! bang! thump! tip! turn! joggle! jolt!—Hold on to your ribs! Look out for the stump! Isn't it fun to go leafing? Isn't it fun to do anything that your heart does with you—even though you do it for a pig?

Just watch the pig as we shake out the bags of leaves. See him caper, spin on his toes, shake himself, and curl his tail. That curl is his laugh. We double up and weep when we laugh hard; but the pig can't weep, and he can't double himself up, so he doubles up his tail. There is where his laugh comes off, curling and kinking in little spasms of pure pig joy!

Boosh! Boosh! he snorts, and darts around the pen like a whirlwind, scattering the leaves in forty ways, to stop short—the shortest stop!—and fall to rooting for acorns.

He was once a long-tusked boar of the forest,—this snow-white, sawed-off, pug-faced little porker of mine—ages and ages ago. But he still remembers the smell of the forest leaves; he still knows the taste of the acorn-mast; he is still wild pig in his soul.

And we were once long-haired, strong-limbed savages who roamed the forest hunting him—ages and ages ago. And we, too, like him, remember the smell of the fallen leaves, and the taste of the forest fruits—and of pig, *roast* pig! And if the pig in his heart is still a wild boar, no less are we, at times, wild savages in our hearts.

Anyhow, for one day in the fall I want to go "leafing." I want to give my pig a taste of acorns, and a big pile of leaves to dive so deep into that he cannot see his pen. I can feel the joy of it myself. No, I do not live in a pen; but then, I might, if once in a while I did not go leafing, did not escape now and then from my little daily round into the wide, wild woods—my ancestral home.

CHAPTER XII

A CHAPTER OF THINGS TO HEAR THIS FALL

I

OU ought to hear the scream of the hen-hawks circling high in the air. In August and September and late into October, if you listen in the open country, you will hear their piercing whistle,—shrill, exultant *scream* comes nearer to describing it,—as they sail and sail a mile away in the sky.

II

You ought to go out upon some mowing hill or field of stubble and hear the crickets, then into the apple orchard and hear the katydids, then into the high grass and bushes along the fence and hear the whole stringed chorus of green grasshoppers, katydids, and crickets. You have heard them all your life; but the trouble is that, because you have heard them so constantly in the autumn, and because one player after another has come gradually into the orchestra, you have taken them as part of the natural course of things and have never really heard them individually, to know what parts they play. Now anybody can hear a lion roar, or a mule bray, or a loon laugh his wild crazy laugh over a silent mountain lake, and know what sound it is; but who can hear a cricket out of doors, or a grasshopper, and know which is which?

III

Did you ever hear a loon laugh? You ought to. I would go a hundred miles to hear that weird, meaningless, melancholy, maniacal laughter of the loon, or great northern diver, as the dusk comes down over some  lonely lake in the wilderness of the far North. From Maine westward to northern Illinois you may listen for him in early autumn; then, when the migration begins, anywhere south to the Gulf of Mexico. You may never hear the call of the bull moose in the northern woods, nor the howl of a coyote on the western prairies, nor the wild *cac, cac, cac* of the soaring eagles, nor the husky *yap, yap, yap* of the fox. But, if you do, "make a note of it," as Captain Cuttle would say; for the tongues that utter this wild language are fast ceasing to speak to us.

IV

One strangely sweet, strangely wild voice that you still

may hear in our old apple orchards, is the whimpering, whinnying voice of the little screech owl. "When night comes," says the bird book, "one may hear the screech owl's tremulous, wailing whistle. It is a weird, melancholy call, welcomed only by those who love Nature's voice, whatever be the medium through which she speaks." Now listen this autumn for the screech owl; listen until the weird, melancholy call *is* welcomed by you, until the shiver that creeps up your back turns off through your hair, as you hear the low plaintive voice speaking to you out of the hollow darkness, out of the softness and the silence of night.

V

You ought to hear the brown leaves rustling under your feet.

"Heaped in the hollows of the grove, the autumn leaves lie dead;
They rustle to the eddying gust, and to the rabbit's tread."

And they should rustle to your tread as well. Scuff along in them where they lie in deep windrows by the side of the road; and hear them also, as the wind gathers them into a whirling flurry and sends them rattling over the fields.

VI

You ought to hear the cry of the blue jay and the caw of the crow in the autumn woods.

> "The robin and the wren are flown, but from the
> shrub the jay,
> And from the wood-top calls the crow through all the
> gloomy day."

Everybody knows those lines of Bryant, because everybody has heard that loud scream of the jay in the lonesome woods, and the *caw, caw, caw* of the sentinel crow from the top of some tall tree. The robins may not be all gone, for I heard and saw a flock of them this year in January; but they are silent now, and so many of the birds have gone, and the woods have become so empty, that the cries of the jay and the crow seem, on a gloomy day, to be the only sounds in all the hollow woods. There could hardly be an autumn for me if I did not hear these two voices speaking—the one with  a kind of warning in its shrill, half-plaintive cry; the other with a message slow and solemn, like the color of its sable coat.

VII

You ought to hear, you ought to *catch*, I should say, a good round scolding from the red squirrel this fall. A red squirrel is always ready to scold you (and doubtless you are always in need of his scolding), but he is never so breathless and emphatic as in the fall. "Whose nuts are these in the woods?" he asks, as

you come up with your stick and bag. "Who found this tree first? Come, get out of here! Get right back to the city and eat peanuts! Come, do you hear? Get out of this!"

No, don't be afraid; he won't "eat you alive"—though I think he might if he were big enough. He won't blow up, either, and burst! He is the kind of fire-cracker that you call a "sizzler"— all sputter and no explosion. But isn't he a tempest! Isn't he a whirlwind! Isn't he a red-coated cyclone! Let him blow! The little scamp, he steals birds' eggs in the summer, they say; but there are none now for him to steal, and the woods are very empty. We need a dash of him on these autumn days, as we need a dash of spice in our food.

In the far western mountains he has a cousin called the Douglas squirrel; and Mr. John Muir calls him "the brightest of all the squirrels I have ever seen, a hot spark of life, making every tree tingle with his prickly toes, a condensed nugget of fresh mountain vigor and valor, as free from disease as a sunbeam. How he scolds, and what faces he makes, all eyes, teeth, and whiskers!"

You must hear him this fall and take your scolding, whether you deserve it or not.

VIII

You ought to hear in the cedars, pines, or spruces the small thin *cheep, cheep, cheep* of the chickadees or the kinglets. You must take a quiet day on the very edge of winter and, in some sunny dip or glade, hear them as they feed and flit about you. They speak in a language differ-ent from that of the crow and the jay. This tiny talk of the kinglet is all friendly and cheerful and personal and confidential, as if you were one of the party and liked spiders' eggs and sunshine and didn't care a snap for the coming winter! In all the vast gray out of doors what bits of winged bravery, what crumbs of feathered cour-age, they seem! One is hardly ready for the winter until he has heard them in the cedars and has been assured that they will stay, no matter how it snows and blows.

IX

You ought to hear, some quiet day or moonlit night in Octo-ber or November, the baying of the hounds as they course the swamps and meadows on the heels of the fox. Strange advice, you say? No, not strange. It is a wild, fierce cry that your fathers heard, and their fathers, and theirs—away on back to the cave days, when life was hardly anything but the hunt, and the dogs were the only tame animal, and the most useful possession, man had. Their deep bass voices have echoed through all the wild forests of our past, and stir within us nowadays wild memories that are good for us again to feel. Stand still, as the baying pack comes bringing the quarry through the forest toward you. The blood will leap in your veins, as the ringing cries lift and fall in the chorus that echoes back from every hollow and hill around; and you will on with the panting pack—will on in the fierce, wild exultation of the chase; for instinctively we are hunters, just as all our ancestors were.

No, don't be afraid. You won't catch the fox.

X

You ought to hear by day—or better, by night—the call of the migrating birds as they pass over, through the sky, on their way to the South. East or west, on the Atlantic or on the Pacific shore, or in the vast valley of the Mississippi, you may hear at night, so high in air that you cannot see the birds, these voices of the passing migrants. *Chink, chink, chink!* will drop the calls of the bobolinks—fine, metallic, starry notes; *honk, honk, honk!* the clarion cry of the wild geese will ring along the aërial way, as they shout to one another and to you, listening far below them on the steadfast earth.

Far away, yonder in the starry vault, far beyond the reach of human eyes, a multitude of feathered folk, myriads of them, are streaming over; armies of them winging down the long highway of the sky from the frozen North, down to the rice fields of the Carolinas, down to the deep tangled jungles of the Amazon, down beyond the cold, cruel reach of winter.

Listen as they hail you from the sky.

CHAPTER XIII

HONK, HONK, HONK!

ONK, *honk, honk!* Out of the silence of the November night, down through the depths of the darkened sky, rang the thrilling call of the passing geese.

Honk, honk, honk! I was out of bed in an instant; but before I had touched the floor, there was a patter of feet in the boys' room, the creak of windows going up, and—silence.

Honk, honk, honk! A mighty flock was coming. The stars shone clear in the far blue; the trees stood dark on the rim of the North; and somewhere between the trees and the stars, somewhere along a pathway running north and south, close up against the distant sky, the wild geese were winging.

Honk, honk, honk! They were overhead. Clear as bugles, round and mellow as falling flute notes, ordered as the tramp of soldiers, fell the *honk, honk, honk*, as the flock in single line, or double like the letter V, swept over and was gone.

We had not seen them. Out of a sound sleep they had summoned us, out of beds with four wooden legs and no wings; and we had heard the wild sky-call, had heard and followed through our open windows, through the dark of the night, up into the blue vault under the light of the stars.

Round and dim swung the earth below us, hushed and asleep in the soft arms of the night. Hill and valley lay close together, farm-land and wood-land, all wrapped in the coverlet of the dark. City and town, like watch fires along the edge of a sleeping camp, burned bright on the rivers and brighter still on the ragged line of shore and sea, for we were far away near the stars. The mountains rose up, but they could not reach us; the white lakes beckoned, but they could not call us down. For the stars were bright, the sky-coast was clear, the wind in our wings was the keen, wild wind of the North, and the call that we heard—ah! who knows the call? Yet, who does not know it—that distant haunting call to fly, fly, fly?

I found myself in my bed the next morning. I found the small boys in their beds. I found the big round sun in the sky that morning and not a star in sight! There was nothing unusual to be seen up there, nothing mysterious at all. But there was something unusual, something mysterious to be seen in the four small faces at the breakfast-table that morning—eyes all full of stars and deep with the far, dark depths of the midnight sky into which they had gazed—into which those four small boys had flown!

We had often heard the geese go over before, but never such a flock as this, never such wild waking clangor, so clear, so far away, so measured, swift, and—gone!

I love the sound of the ocean surf, the roar of a winter gale in the leafless woods, the sough of the moss-hung cypress in the dark southern swamps. But no other voice of Nature is so strangely, deeply thrilling to me as the *honk, honk, honk* of the passing geese.

For what other voice, heard nowadays, of beast or bird is so wild and free and far-resounding? Heard in the solemn silence of the night, the notes fall as from the stars, a faint and far-off salutation, like the call of sentinels down the picket line—"All's well! All's well!" Heard in the open day, when you can see the winged wedge splitting through the dull gray sky, the notes seem to cleave the dun clouds, driven down by the powerful wing-beats where the travelers are passing high and far beyond the reach of our guns.

The sight of the geese going over in the day, and the sound of their trumpetings, turn the whole world of cloud and sky into a wilderness, as wild and primeval a wilderness as that distant forest of the far Northwest where the howl of wolves is still heard by the trappers. Even that wilderness, however, is passing; and perhaps no one of us will ever hear the howl of wolves in the hollow snow-filled forests, as many of our parents have heard. But the *honk* of the wild geese going over we should all hear, and our children should hear; for this flock of wild creatures we have in our hands to preserve.

The wild geese breed in the low, wet marshes of the half-frozen North, where, for a thousand years to come they will not interfere with the needs of man. They pass over our northern and middle states and spend the winter in the rivers, marshes, and lagoons of the South, where, for another thousand years to come, they can do little, if any, harm to man, but rather good.

But North and South, and all along their journey back and forth, they are shot for sport and food. For the wild geese cannot make this thousand-mile flight without coming down to rest and eat; and wherever that descent is made, there is pretty sure to be a man with a gun on the watch.

Here, close to my home, are four ponds; and around the sides of each of them are "goose blinds"—screens made of cedar and pine boughs fixed into the shore, behind which the gunners lie in wait. More than that, out upon the surface of the pond are geese swimming, but tied so that they cannot escape—geese that have been raised in captivity and placed there to lure the flying wild flocks down. Others, known as "flyers," are kept within the blind to be let loose when a big flock is seen approaching—to fly out and mingle with them and decoy them to the pond. These "flyers" are usually young birds and, when thrown out upon their wings, naturally come back, bringing the wild flock with them, to their fellows fastened in the pond.

A weary flock comes winging over, hungry, and looking for a place to rest. Instantly the captive geese out on the pond see them and set up a loud honking. The flying flock hear them and begin to descend. Then they see one (tossed from the blind) coming on to meet them, and they circle lower to the pond, only to fall before a fury of shots that pour from behind the blind.

Those of the flock that are not killed rise frightened and bewildered to fly to the opposite shore, where other guns riddle them, the whole flock sometimes perishing within the ring of fire!

Such shooting is a crime because it is unfair, giving the creature no chance to exercise his native wit and caution. The fun of hunting, as of any sport, is in playing the game—the danger, the exercise, the pitting of limb against limb, wit against wit, patience against patience; not in a heap of carcasses, the dead and bloody weight of mere meat!

If the hunter would only play fair with the wild goose, shoot him (the wild Canada goose) only along the North Carolina coast, where he passes the winter, then there would be no danger of the noble bird's becoming extinct. And the hunter then would know what real sport is, and what a long-headed, far-sighted goose the wild goose really is—for there are few birds with his cunning and alertness.

Along the Carolina shore the geese congregate in vast numbers; and when the day is calm, they ride out into the ocean after feeding, so far off shore that no hunter could approach them. At night they come in for shelter across the bars, sailing into the safety of the inlets and bays for a place to sleep. If the wind rises, and a storm blows up, then they must remain in the pools and water-holes, where the hunter has a chance to take them. Only here, where the odds, never even, are not all against the birds, should the wild geese be hunted.

With the coming of March there is a new note in the clamor of the flocks, a new restlessness in their movements; and, before the month is gone, many mated pairs of the birds have flocked together and are off on their far northern journey to the icy lakes of Newfoundland and the wild, bleak marshes of Labrador.

Honk, honk, honk! Shall I hear them going over,—going northward,—as I have heard them going southward this fall? Winter comes down in their wake. There is the clang of the cold in their trumpeting, the closing of iron gates, the bolting of iron doors for the long boreal night. They pass and leave the forests empty, the meadows brown and sodden, the rivers silent, the bays and lakes close sealed. Spring will come up with them on their return; and their *honk, honk, honk* will waken the frogs from their oozy slumbers and stir every winter sleeper to the very circle of the Pole.

Honk, honk, honk! Oh, may I be awake to hear you, ye strong-winged travelers on the sky, when ye go over northward, calling the sleeping earth to waken, calling all the South to follow you through the broken ice-gates of the North!

Honk, honk, honk! The wild geese are passing—southward!

NOTES AND SUGGESTIONS

CHAPTER I

TO THE TEACHER

Go yourself frequently into the fields and woods, or into the city parks, or along the water front—anywhere so that you can touch nature directly, and look and listen for yourselves. Don't try to teach what you do not know, and there is nothing in this book that you cannot know, for the *lesson* to be taught in each chapter is a spiritual lesson, not a number of bare facts. This spiritual lesson you must first learn before you can teach it—must *feel*, I should say; and a single thoughtful excursion alone into the autumn fields will give you possession of it. And what is the lesson in this chapter? Just this: that the strong growths of summer, the ripening of seeds and fruits, the languid lazy spirit, and the pensive signs of coming autumn are all the manifold preparations of nature for a fresh outburst of life with the coming of spring.

FOR THE PUPIL

PAGE 9

The clock of the year strikes one: When, in the daytime, the clock strikes one, the hour of noon is past; the afternoon begins. On the 21st of June the clock of the year strikes twelve—noon!

By late July the clock strikes one—the noon hour is past! Summer is gone; autumn—the afternoon of the year—begins.

going "creepy-creep": In the quiet of some July day in fields or woods, listen to the stirring of the insects and other small wood creatures. All summer long they are going about their business, but in the midst of stronger noises we are almost deaf to their world of little sounds.

Page 12

begins to shift: Why is the oak's shadow likely to be "round" at noon? What causes the shadow to "shift"; or move? In which direction would it move?

falls a yellow leaf from a slender birch near by... small flock of robins from a pine... swallows were gathering upon the telegraph wires: Next summer, note the exact date on which you first see signs of autumn—the first falling of the leaves, the first gathering of birds for their southern trip. Most of the migrating birds go in flocks for the sake of companionship and protection.

chewink (named from his call, chē-wink´; accent on second, not on first, syllable, as in some dictionaries) or ground robin, or towhee or joree; one of the finch family. You will know him by his saying "chewink" and by his vigorous scratching among the dead leaves, and by his red-brown body and black head and neck.

vireo (vīr´-ē-ō): the red-eyed vireo, the commonest of the vireo family; often called "Preacher"; builds the little hanging nest from a small fork on a bush or tree so low often that you can look into it.

fiery notes of the scarlet tanager (tăn´-a-jēr): His notes are loud and strong, and he is dressed in fiery red clothes and sings on the fieriest of July days.

resonant song of the indigo bunting: or indigo-bird, one of the finch family. He sings from the very tip of a tree as if to get up close under the dome of the sky. Indeed, his notes seem to strike against it and ring down to us; for there is a peculiar ringing quality to them, as if he were singing to you from inside a great copper kettle.

scarlet tanager by some accident: The tanager arrives among the last of the birds in the spring, and builds late; but, if you find a nest in July or August, it is pretty certain to be a second nest, the first having been destroyed somehow—a too frequent occurrence with all birds.

half-fledged cuckoos: The cuckoo also is a very late builder. I have more than once found its eggs in July.

red wood-lily: Do you know the wood-lily, or the "wild orange-red lily" as some call it (*Lilium philadelphicum*)? It is found from New England to North Carolina and west to Missouri, but only on hot, dry, sandy ground, whereas the turk's-cap and the wild yellow lily are found only where the ground is rich and moist.

low mouldy moss: Bring to school a flake, as large as your hand, of the kind of lichen you think this may be. Some call it "reindeer moss."

sweet-fern: Put a handful of sweet-fern (*Myrica asplenifolia*) in your pocket, a leaf or two in your book; and whenever you pass it in the fields, pull it through your fingers for the odor. Sweet gale and bayberry are its two sweet relatives.

milkweed, boneset, peppermint, turtle-head, joe-pye-weed, jewel-weed, smartweed, and budding goldenrod: Go down to the nearest meadow stream and gather for school as many of these flowers as you can find. Examine their seeds.

wind is a sower going forth to sow: Besides the winds what other seed-scatterers do you know? They are many and very interesting.

PAGE 14

"Over the fields where the daisies grow...."
From "Thistledown" in a volume of poems called "Summer-Fallow," by Charles Buxton Going.

seed-souls of thistles and daisies and fall dandelions seeking new bodies for themselves in the warm soil of Mother Earth: On your country walks, watch to see where such seeds have been caught, or have fallen. They will be washed down into the earth by rain and snow. If you can mark the place, go again next spring to see for yourself if they have risen in "new bodies" from the earth.

sweet pepper-bush: The sweet pepper-bush is also called white alder and clethra.

chickadees: Stand stock-still upon meeting a flock of chicka-dees and see how curious they become to know you. You may know the chickadee by its tiny size, its gray coat, black cap and throat, its saying "chick-a-dee," and its plaintive call of "phœbe" in three distinct syllables.

PAGE 15

clock strikes twelve: As we have thought of midsummer as the hour from twelve to one in the day, so the dead of winter seems by comparison the twelve o'clock of midnight.

shimmering of the spiders' silky balloons: It is the curious habit of many of the spiders to travel, especially in the fall, by throwing skeins of silky web into the air, which the breezes catch and carry up, while the spiders, like balloonists, hang in their web ropes below and sail away.

CHAPTER II

TO THE TEACHER

I have chosen the fox in this chapter to illustrate this very interesting and striking fact that wild animals, birds and beasts, thrive in the neighborhood of man if given the least protection; for if the fox holds his own (as surely he does) in the very gates of one of the largest cities in the United States, how easy it should be for us to preserve for generations yet the birds and smaller animals! I might have written a very earnest chapter on the need for every pupil's joining the Audubon Society and the Animal Rescue League; but young pupils, no less than their elders, hate to be preached to. So I have recounted a series of short narratives, trusting to the suggestions of the chapter, and to the quiet comment of the teacher to do the good work. *Every pupil a protector of wild life is the moral.*

FOR THE PUPIL

There are two species of foxes in the eastern states—the gray fox, common from New Jersey southward, and the larger red fox, so frequent here in New England and northward, popularly known at Reynard. Far up under the Arctic circle lives the little white or Arctic fox, so valuable for its fur; and in California still another species known as the coast fox. The so-called silver or blue, or black, or cross fox, is only the red fox with a blackish or bluish coat.

Mullein Hill: the name of the author's country home in Hingham, Massachusetts. The house is built on the top of a wooded ridge looking down upon the tops of the orchard trees and away over miles of meadow and woodland to the Blue Hills, and at night to the lights that flash in Boston Harbor. Years before the house was built the ridge was known as Mullein Hill because of the number and size of the mulleins (*Verbascum Thapsus*) that grew upon its sides and top.

mowing-field: a New England term for a field kept permanently in grass for hay.

grubby acres: referring to the grubs of various beetles found in the soil and under the leaves of its woodland.

BB: the name of shot about the size of sweet pea seed.

Pigeon Henny's coop: a pet name for one of the hens that looked very much like a pigeon.

shells: loaded cartridges used in a breech-loading gun.

bead drew dead: when the little metal ball on the end of the gun-barrel, used to aim by, showed that the gun was pointing directly at the fox.

the mind in the wild animal world: how the animals may really feel when being chased, namely, not frightened to death, as we commonly think, but perhaps cool and collected, taking the chase as a matter of course, even enjoying it.

The Chase: The sound of the hunting is likened to a chorus of singing voices; the changing sounds, as when the pack emerges from thick woods into open meadow, being likened to the various measures of the musical score; the whole musical composition or chorus being called *The Chase*.

PAGE 26

dead heat: a race between two or more horses or boats where two of the racers come out even, neither winning.

Flood: Why spelled with a capital? What flood is meant?

PAGE 27

hard-pressed fox had narrowly won his way: In spite of the author's attempt to shoot the fox that was stealing his chickens do you think the author would be glad if there were no foxes in his woods? How do they add interest to his out of doors? What other things besides chickens do they eat? Might it not be that their destruction of woodchucks (for they eat woodchucks) and mice and muskrats quite balances their killing of poultry? (The author thinks so.)

CHAPTER III

TO THE TEACHER

The thought in this chapter is evident, namely, that love for the out of doors is dependent upon knowledge of the out of doors. The more we *know* and the better we *understand*, the more perfect and marvelous nature seems and the more lovely. The toadfish *looks* loathly, but upon closer study he becomes very interesting, even admirable—one of the very foundations of real love. So, as a teacher and as a lover of nature, be careful never to use the words "ugly" or "nasty" or "loathly"; never shrink from a toad; never make a wry face at a worm; never show that you are having a nervous fit at a snake; for it all argues a lack of knowledge and understanding. All life, from Man to the Amœba, is one long series of links in a golden chain, one succession of wonderful life-histories, each vastly important, all making up the divinely beautiful world of life which our lives crown, but of which we are only a part, and, perhaps, no more important a part than the toadfish.

FOR THE PUPIL

The toadfish of this story is *Batrachus tau*, sometimes called oyster-fish or sapo. The fishing-frog or angler is by some called toadfish, as is also the swell-fish or common puffer of the Atlantic Coast.

PAGE 28

Buzzards Bay: Where is Buzzards Bay? Do you know Whittier's beautiful poem, *The Prayer of Agassiz*, which begins:—

> "On the isle of Penikese
> Ringed about by sapphire seas."

Where is Penikese? What waters are those "sapphire seas," and what was Agassiz doing there?

PAGE 29

Davy Jones: Who is Davy Jones? Look him up under *Jones, Davy*, in your dictionary of *Proper Names*. Get into the "looking up" habit. Never let anything in your reading, that you do not understand, go unlooked up.

Old Man of the Sea: Look him up too. Are he and Davy Jones any relation?

It was really a fish: What names do you think of that might fit this fish?

PAGE 32

coarsely marbled with a darker hue: What is the meaning of marbled?

PAGE 33

covered with water: The author means that the *rock* is not always covered with water, not the *hole* under the rock. Of course the hole is always built so that it is full of water, else the fish would perish at low tide.

PAGE 35

love the out of doors with all your mind: Do you know what is meant by loving the out of doors with your mind? Just this: that while you feel (with your heart) the beauty of a star, at the same time you know (with your mind) that that particular star, let us say, is the Pole Star, the guide to the sailors on the seas; that it is also only one of a vast multitude of stars each one of which has its place in the heavens, its circuit or path through the skies, its part in the whole orderly universe—a *thought* so vast and wonderful that we cannot comprehend it. All this it means to love with our minds. Without minds a star to us is only a point of light, as to Peter Bell

> "A primrose by the river's brim
> A yellow primrose was to him
> And it was nothing more."

Does the toadfish become anything more than a mere toadfish in a shoe before the end of the chapter?

in the toadfish's shoe: What does the author mean by asking you to put yourself in the toadfish's shoe? Only this: to try, even with the humblest of creatures, to share sympathetically their lives with them. The best way to do this with man as well as with toadfish is to learn about their lives.

CHAPTER IV

TO THE TEACHER

There are several practical uses to which you can put this chapter, and the similar chapters, VII and XII: they can be made the purpose for field excursions with the class. Such excursions might be quite impossible for many a teacher in school hours; and we know how the exacting duties overcrowd the after-school hours; but one field excursion each season of the year, no matter how precious your time, would do more for you and your class than many books about nature read inside your four plastered walls. Better the books than nothing; but take the book and go with your pupils into the real out of doors.

Again, you can make these chapters a kind of nature test, asking each pupil to try to see each of the things suggested here; or, if these do not chance to be the sights characteristic of the autumn in your region, then such sights as are characteristic. So the chapter can serve as a kind of field guide to the pupil, and a kind of test of his knowledge of nature.

Again, you can make each item mentioned here the subject for a short composition direct from the pupil's experience—the only kind of subject for him to write upon. Or make each item (say, No. IV, the Ballooning Spiders) the beginning for a short course of study or collateral reading for the individual pupil particularly interested in spiders!

CHAPTER V

TO THE TEACHER

The real point of this story (but first of all it is a story and should not be spoiled with any moral) is the thought in the lines:—

"There were thousands of persons who could have gold eggs if they cared. But eagles' eggs! Money could not buy such a sight as this." Which means, that the simple joys of the out of doors, and the possession of youth and health, are better than any joys that money can create, and more precious possessions than all the money in the world can buy. One can get all the thrilling sensations of height by standing up in a quaking eagle's nest sixty feet from the ground, that one can possibly get from the top of the Eiffel Tower or on the peak of Mount Washington, or from a flying-machine among the clouds. And then who among the rich of the world ever saw eagles' eggs in a nest, or had eagles dig him with their talons? To be alive to all the wonder of the life, to all the beauty of the world about us, is the very secret of living. An eagle's nest to climb into is as good as a flying-machine.

Take occasion, too, at the end of the story to say how much better, how much more interesting, an act it was to leave the eggs to hatch than to rob the nest and thus destroy two young eagles. Some years later, for instance, two young eagles were taken from a neighboring nest and were sent to the Zoölogical Gardens at Philadelphia, where they may still be living for thousands of visitors each year to see. Who knows but that one of the parents of these two captive birds may have been in the eggs laid back by the boy in that nest?

FOR THE PUPIL

PAGE 44

Maurice River Cove: Where is Maurice River Cove? What is the Cove famous for?

great eagle's nest: Look up the habits of the bald eagle in some natural history. Is he a very great enemy to man? If a pair of the noble birds lived in your neighborhood would you want their nest destroyed and the birds shot? Do you know the story of "Old Abe"? Look that up also.

PAGE 45

scream of a wild cat: The wild cat is still to be found throughout the United States wherever the country is very wild and wooded. Its cry or scream is an indescribable thrill that shoots cold all over you, freezing fast in the roots of your hair.

mud-hens: The mud-hen or American coot, a dark bluish slate-colored bird of the marshes about the size of a large bantam, with an ivory-white bill and peculiar lobed toes, instead of webbed like a duck's.

eyrie: What does the word mean? Are there any other ways of spelling it?

PAGE 46

size of a small haystack: This is no exaggeration. From one nest of a fish hawk (and this nest was probably built first by a fish hawk) that blew down from the top of an old house chimney in the Maurice River Marshes, the author knew six one-horse cartloads of loose sticks to be taken.

PAGE 47

such a sight as this: Have you ever seen a sunset more gorgeous than any artist could paint and any rich man could buy? Ever had a smell of trailing arbutus that no perfumer could equal, that all the money in the world could not create? Old Midas had a golden touch and turned his daughter into gold. Was he not more than willing to be the poorest man in his kingdom if only he might be rid of the fatal touch, be a natural man again and have his loving little daughter a natural child again? To be your natural selves, and to enjoy your beautiful natural world is better than to be anything else, or to have anything else, in the world.

CHAPTER VI

TO THE TEACHER

We hear so much of the drudgery of farm life, of its dreariness, and meagre living that this chapter, aside from its picture of cheer and plenty, should be made the text for a good deal of comment upon the many other phases of farm life that make for the fullest kind of existence; namely, the independence of the farmer; the vast and interesting variety of his work; his personal contact with domestic animals, his fruit-trees, garden, and fields of grain; his intimate acquaintance with the weather; his great resourcefulness in meeting insect plagues, blights, and droughts; his out-of-door life that makes him strong and long-lived, etc., etc.

If you are a country teacher it is one of your great missions to show the boys that they should stay upon the farm, or rather that the farm is a good place to stay on for life; if you are a city teacher it should be your mission to head many a boy countryward for life with the understanding that it requires more sound sense and resourcefulness to make a successful farmer than it does to make a bank president.

FOR THE PUPIL

end of the outdoors: The fall plowing, even the digging of the ditches—all the work in the soil is about over by Thanksgiving when the ground begins to freeze.

crib-house: Where the writer lived as a boy the corn was husked and left in the ear and stored in long, narrow houses built of beveled slats spaced about half an inch apart to allow the wind free play, but like the thin slats of a shutter so arranged that the rain ran down and, except in a driving wind, did not wet the grain.

"spring-house": Spring-houses took the place of modern ice-chests, being little cupboard-like houses well ventilated and screened, built near the farmhouse and usually over a spring of water that kept the milk and other contents cool.

battened: Is this a "land" term or a "sea" term? What does it mean? Look it up and report.

the swallows: These were the barn swallows—the beautiful swallows with the long, finely-forked tail. You will always know them on the wing by the brown breast and *fine* forked tail.

worm-fence: A worm-fence is built of rails laid one on top of the other, running zigzag, each corner held together by two upright stakes, set in the ground and crossed just above the next-to-the-top rail. The top rail is laid in the crotch of the two stakes.

turn-o'-lane: name of a very excellent old-fashioned apple that got its name from the fact that the original tree of the kind grew at a turn of the lane—the writer does not know whose lane.

double-hived: It is customary to cover beehives with newspapers, then slip an outside box down over papers and all to keep the swarm from the cutting cold winds of winter. Bees are frequently brought into the cellar for the winter in northern latitudes.

put on an extra coat, and turned their collars up about their ears: What does the writer mean?

changed their roost from the ridge-pole: Turkeys roost high; but the ridge-pole of the crib-house used to be too cold in the dead of winter, so they would change to the more protected apple-tree, still roosting high, however.

pearmain: name of a "summer" apple in New Jersey; of a winter apple in this section of Massachusetts.

garden of box: the box bush.

bleeding-hearts: an old-fashioned flower; a low shrub with pendent blossoms shaped like a heart.

creeper: the Virginia creeper, or woodbine.

PAGE 56

"template" stove: from template or templet, a strip of sheet iron used in boiler-making. A simple long stove made of a single piece of sheet iron, bent like an inverted U, and riveted to a cast iron bottom. It had a single door in the front; and burnt pieces of wood about two feet long. Often called "tenplate" stove.

seven of us alone: seven brothers and sisters in the writer's family.

flats: Describe the outside appearance of a city "flat," and also the inside if you have ever been in a flat. Is it like a farmhouse?

kitchenette: What kind of a kitchen is a kitchen*ette*?

neither a farm nor a city home: By which the writer means

a farm in the ordinary sense of land cultivated for a living. His is a home only, with several acres around it, largely in woods and grass.

Page 57

"*Bucksy*": the invented name of a little Indian hero about whom the writer tells stories to his little boys.

CHAPTER VII

TO THE TEACHER

Suggestions as to the practical uses to which this chapter can be put may be gathered from the notes to chapter IV and chapter XII, each of which is similar to this one.

CHAPTER VIII

TO THE TEACHER

This chapter and the next (chapter IX) should be taken together as a single study of the provision of nature against the severity of winter's cold, chapter VIII being a detailed account of one creature's preparations, while chapter IX follows, showing how the foresight and care obtain even among the plants and trees. The two chapters together should give the pupils a glad thought for winter, should utterly change their conventional language and feeling for it as a time of *death*. And instead of lamenting the season as a necessary evil, you must show them that it is to be welcomed as a period of sleep for nature from which she will waken in all the freshness of a springtime such as is nowhere to be had outside of the temperate zone. "It is not always May," wails the poet; but ask them: Who wants it always

May? We want the variety, the contrasts of our four seasons, and as to winter, let the North Wind blow at will, redden our cheeks, quicken our step, put purpose into our wills and—it won't starve us; for we, too, like the muskrat, are provided for.

FOR THE PUPIL

If there is a muskrat house or village of houses in your neighborhood, report to the class, or better, take teacher and class, as soon as freezing weather comes, to see it. Go out yourselves and try to see the muskrats plastering their walls on one of the bright October nights.

PAGE 68

muskrats combine: The author has frequently found as many as six rats in a single house; but whether all of these helped in the building or not, he is unable to say.

winter house: If the house is undisturbed (as when situated out in a stumpy pond) it will stand for years, the rats dwelling in it the year around.

pick and shovel: What is meant by a fox's "pick and shovel"?

Lupton's Pond: the name of a little wood-walled pond that the author haunted as a boy.

> "The best-laid schemes o' mice and men
> Gang aft agley."

Learn this poem ("To A Mouse") by heart. Burns is the author.

PAGE 69

very much alike: Name some other respects in which animals and men are alike in their lives. What famous line in the poem just quoted is it that makes men and mice very closely related?

bottom of the house: Down in the very foundation walls of

the muskrat's house are two runways or "doors" that open under water and so far under that they rarely if ever freeze. See picture of such a house with its door in the author's "Wild Life Near Home," page 174.

PAGE 70

tepee: What is a tepee?

juicy and pink and tender: The muskrats eat grass stems and roots, so that under the water near the lodge you will often find in winter little stacks of these tender pink stems and roots ready for eating—much as the beaver stores up sticks of tender bark under the water near his lodge for food when the ice forms overhead.

Winter is coming: Are you glad or sorry? Are you ready?

CHAPTER IX

TO THE TEACHER

Let the pupils continue this list of examples of winter preparations by watching and observing for themselves. Every field, every tree, every roadside, will reveal the work done or going on under their eyes. Without preaching you may draw many an interesting and telling parallel with their own preparation—in school for instance.

FOR THE PUPIL

PAGE 71

> "The north wind doth blow,
> And we shall have snow,
> And what will the Robin do then,
> Poor thing?"

121

Where does the verse come from? Mother Goose? Yes, but who was she?

Chipmunk: Our little striped ground squirrel, interesting because he has cheek-pouches and thus forms a link between the arboreal squirrels (gray squirrels, etc.) and the ground squirrels or spermophiles, of which the beautiful little thirteen-lined squirrel of the prairies is an example.

Whitefoot, the wood mouse: The white-footed or wood mouse or deer mouse.

Not so much as a bug or a single beetle's egg has he stored: Why not, seeing that these are his food?

a piece of suet for him on a certain lilac bush: Whose bush might it be? Is there a piece on yours?

upon the telegraph-wires were the swallows—the first sign that the getting ready for winter has begun: What kind or kinds of swallows? Have you any earlier sign?

Page 73

the few creatures that find food and shelter in the snow: Name four of the *animals* that so find their food and shelter. Are there any others? Look them up.

there will be suffering and death: In your tramps afield this winter look out for signs of suffering. There are many little things that you can do to lessen it—a little seed scattered, a piece of suet nailed up on a tree, a place cleared in the snow where gravel stones can be picked up.

or even three hundred pounds of honey: By not allowing the bees to swarm, and thus divide their strength, bee-keepers often get more than three hundred pounds of comb-honey (in the little pound boxes or sections) from a single hive. The bees

themselves require only about twenty to twenty-five pounds
to carry them through the winter.

PAGE 74

the witch-hazels: The witch-hazels do not yield honey so far
as the author has observed. Suppose you watch this autumn
to see if the honey-bees (do you know a honey-bee when you
see *her*?) visit it. Whence comes this quotation? From which
poem of Bryant's:—

"when come the calm, mild days."

put on their storm-doors: In modern bee-hives there is a mov-
able board in front upon which the bees alight when entering
the hive; this can be so turned as to make a large doorway for
the summer, and a small entrance for the cold winter.

whole drove of forty-six woodchucks: The author at one time
had forty-six inhabited woodchuck holes on his farm.

PAGE 75

as Bobolink among the reeds of the distant Orinoco: The
bobolink winters even farther south—beyond the banks of
the Amazon.

to sleep until dawn of spring: What is the name for this strange
sleeping? What other American animals do it? Name three.

PAGE 76

frogs frozen into the middle of solid lumps of ice: Of course,
this was never done intentionally: each time the frogs were
forgotten and left in the laboratory, where they froze.

PAGE 77

they seem to have given up the struggle at once...: This may not
be the explanation. One of the author's friends suggests that
it may have been caused by exposure, due to their having been

frightened in the night from their usual bed and thus forced to roost where they could until morning.

timothy: "Herd's-grass" or "English hay"—as it is sometimes called in New England.

plenty for the birds: What are the "weeds" made for? You growl when you are set to pulling them in the garden. What are they made for? Can you answer?

CHAPTER X

TO THE TEACHER

Perhaps you are in a crowded school-room in the heart of a great city. What can you do for your pupils there? But what *can't* you do? You have a bit of sky, a window surely, an old tin can for earth, a sprig of something to plant—and surely you have English sparrows behind the rain pipe or shutter! You may have the harbor too, and water-front with its gulls and fish, and the fish stores with their windows full of the sea. You have the gardens and parks, burial-grounds and housetops, bird stores, museums—why, bless you, you have the hand-organ man and his monkey; you have—but I have mentioned enough. It is a hungry little flock that you have to feed, too, and no teacher can ask more.

FOR THE PUPIL

PAGE 79

An English sparrow: Make a long and careful study of the sparrows that nest about you. If you live in the country try to drive them away from the bluebird house and the martin-boxes. The author does not advise boys and girls to do any killing, but carefully pulling down a sparrow's nest with eggs in it—if you are *sure* it is a sparrow's nest—is kindness, he believes, to the other, more useful birds. Yet only yesterday, August 17th, he saw a male sparrow bring moth after moth to its young in a hole in one of the timbers of a bridge from which the author was fishing. It is not easy to say just what our duty is in this matter.

PAGE 80

clack of a guinea going to roost: The guinea-fowl as it goes to roost frequently sets up a clacking that can be heard half a mile away.

an ancient cemetery in the very heart of Boston: The cemetery was the historic King's Chapel on Tremont Street, Boston. Some of the elm trees have since been cut down.

Cubby Hollow: a small pond near the author's boyhood home, running, after a half-mile course through the woods, into Lupton's Pond, which falls over a dam into the meadows of Cohansey Creek.

on the water: What water is it that surrounds so large a part of the City of Boston?

PAGE 81

the shuttered buildings: Along some of the streets, especially in the wholesale district, the heavy iron shutters, closed against the high walls of the buildings, give the deserted streets a solemn, almost a forbidding aspect.

facing the wind: like an anchored boat, offering the least possible resistance to the storm.

out of doors lies very close about you, as you hurry down a crowded city street: Opportunities for watching the wild things, for seeing and hearing the things of nature, cannot be denied you even in the heart of the city, if you have an eye for such

things. Read Bradford Torrey's "Birds on Boston Common,"
or the author's "Birds from a City Roof" in the volume called
"Roof and Meadow."

CHAPTER XI

TO THE TEACHER

This is a chapter on the large wholesomeness of contact
with nature; that even the simple, humble tasks out of doors
are attended with a freedom and a naturalness that restore one
to his real self by putting him into his original primitive envi-
ronment and by giving him an original primitive task to do.

Then, too, how good a thing it is to have something alive
and responsive to work for—if only a goat or a pig! Take occasion to read to the class Lamb's essay on Roast Pig—even fifth
grade pupils will get a lasting picture from it.

Again—and this is the apparent purpose of the chapter—
how impossible it is to go into the woods with anything—a
hay-rake—and not find the woods interesting!

FOR THE PUPIL

PAGE 83

the unabridged dictionary: What does "unabridged" mean?

hay-rig: a simple farm wagon with a "rigging" put on for
carting hay.

cord wood: wood cut into four-foot lengths to be cut up
smaller for burning in the stove. What are the dimensions of
a cord of wood?

PAGE 84

through the cold gray of the maple swamp below you, peers the face of Winter: What does one see in a maple swamp at this time of year that looks like the "face of winter." Think.

he that gathers leaves for his pig spreads a blanket of down over his own winter bed: How is this meant to be taken?

round at the barn: It is a common custom with farmers to make this nightly round in order to see that the stock is safe for the night. Were you ever in a barn at night where the horses were still munching hay, and the cattle rattling their stanchions and horns? Recall the picture in Whittier's "Snow-Bound."

PAGE 85

diameters: the unit of measure in the "field" or the lens of the microscope, equivalent to "times."

white-footed wood mouse: Text should read *or* wood mouse. There are other wood mice, but Whitefoot is known as the wood mouse.

gives at the touch: an idiom, meaning *moves* back, gives way.

red-backed salamander: very common under stones; his scientific name is *Plethodon erythronolus.*

His "red" salamander: Read chapter V in "Pepacton," by Burroughs. His salamander is the red triton, *Spelerpes ruber.*

PAGE 86

dull ears: Our ears are dulled by the loud and ceaseless noises of our city life, so that we cannot hear the small voices of nature that doubtless many of the wild creatures are capable of hearing.

tiny tree-frog, Pickering's hyla: the one who peeps so shrill from the meadows in spring.

"skirl": a Scotch term; see "Tam O'Shanter," by Burns: "He screwed the pipes and gart them skirl."

bunches of Christmas fern: Gathered all through the winter here in the ledges about Mullein Hill by the florists for floral pieces.

PAGE 88

yellow-jacket's nest: one of the Vespa Wasps, *Vespa Germanica*. Read the first chapter of "Wasps Social and Solitary," by G. W. and E. G. Peckham.

PAGE 89

long-tusked boar of the forest: The wild boar, the ancestor of our domestic pigs is still to be found in the great game preserves in European forests; in this country only in zoölogical gardens.

live in a pen: How might one, though living in a big modern house, well furnished and ordered, still make a "pen" of it only.

CHAPTER XII

TO THE TEACHER

Notice again that in the three chapters on things to see and do and hear a few of the *characteristic* sights and sounds and doings have been mentioned. Let the whole teaching of these three chapters be to quicken the pupil to look for and listen for the dominant, characteristic sights and sounds of the season, as he must be trained to look for and listen for the characteristic notes and actions of individual things—birds, animals, flowers. If, for instance, his eye catches the galloping, waving motion of the woodpecker's flight, if his ear is trained to distinguish the rappings of the same bird on a hollow limb or resonant rail, then the pupil *knows* that bird and has clues to what is strange in his plumage, his anatomy, his habits, his family traits.

The world outdoors is all a confusion until we know how to separate and distinguish things; and there is no better train-

128

ing for this than to get in the way of looking and listening for what is characteristic.

Each locality differs, however, to some extent in its wild life; so that some of the *sounds* in this chapter may need to have others substituted to meet those differences. Remember that *you* are the teacher, not the book. The book is but a suggestion. You begin where it leaves off; you fill out where it is lacking. A good book is a very good thing; but a good teacher is a very much better thing.

FOR THE PUPIL

Now do not stuff cotton in your ears as soon as you have heard these ten sounds; or, what amounts to the same thing, do not stop listening. If you do only what the book says and nothing else, learn just the day's lesson and nothing more, your teacher may think you a very "good scholar," but I will tell you that you are a poor student of nature. The woods are full of sounds—voices, songs, whisperings—that are to be heard when none of these ten are speaking.

PAGES 90 AND 91

hear their piercing whistle: the husky yap, yap, yap of the fox: It is usually the young hawks in the fall that whistle, as it is usually the young foxes in the summer and fall that bark.

> "Heaped in the hollows of the grove, the autumn leaves lie
>   dead;
> They rustle to the eddying gust, and to the rabbit's tread."
> "The robin and the wren are flown, but from the shrub
>   the jay,
> And from the wood-top calls the crow through all the
>   gloomy day."

Study this whole poem ("The Death of the Flowers," by Bryant) for its excellent natural history. Could the poet have written it had he been ignorant of nature? Can you appreciate it all unless you, too, have heard these sounds, so that the poem can sound them again to you as you read? Nature is not only interesting for herself; but also absolutely necessary for you to know if you would know and love poetry.

the one with a kind of warning in its shrill, half-plaintive cry; the other with a message slow and solemn: What is the warning, would you say, in the scream of the jay? the solemn message in the caw of the crow?

cave days: Cave days mean those prehistoric times in the history of man, when he lived in caves and subsisted almost wholly upon the flesh of wild animals killed with his rude stone weapons.

to the deep tangled jungles of the Amazon: Some of the birds go even farther south—away into Patagonia at the end of the southern hemisphere. There is no more interesting problem, no more thrilling sight in all nature, than this of the migrating birds—the little warblers flying from Brazil to Labrador for the few weeks of summer, there to rear their young and start back again on the long, perilous journey!

CHAPTER XIII

TO THE TEACHER

Let the chapter be read aloud by one pupil, with as much feeling as possible to the paragraph beginning, "I love the sound of the surf," etc.; for this part is story, action, movement. Do not try to *teach* anything in this half. Let some other thoughtful pupil read the next section as far as, *"Honk, honk, honk,"* beginning the third paragraph from the end. This contains the lesson, the moral, and if you stop anywhere to talk about bird-protection, do it here. Let a third pupil read the rest of the chapter. Better than a moral lesson directly taught (and such lessons are much like doses of castor oil) will be the touching of the child's imagination by the picture of the long night-flight high up in the clouds. Read them "To a Water Fowl," by Bryant; and also some good account of migration like that by D. Lange ("The Great Tidal Waves of Bird-Life") in the *Atlantic Monthly* for August, 1909. Read to them Audubon's account of the wild goose, in his "Birds."

FOR THE PUPIL

PAGE 98

followed through our open windows: "followed" how? Must one have wings or a flying-machine in order to "follow" the wild geese?

Round and dim swung the earth below us....: What is the picture? It is seen from what point of view?

the call to fly, fly, fly: Did you ever feel the call to fly? Ever wish you had wings? Ever start and run as Mowgli did, or long to get up and go somewhere as the pilgrims did in the Canterbury Tales?

PAGE 99

in our hands to preserve: Do you belong to the Audubon Society, to the "Grange," or to any of the organizations that are trying to protect and preserve the birds? And are you doing all you can in your neighborhood to protect them?

PAGE 100

not in a heap of carcasses, the dead and bloody weight of mere meat: We may be hunters by instinct; we may love the chase, and we may like to kill things. But do you think that means we ought to, or that we any longer may, kill things? No; bird life has become so scarce that even if we do want to, it is now our duty to give over such sport in the larger interests of the whole country, and try to find a higher, finer kind of pleasure,—as we can in trying to photograph, or "shoot" with the camera, a bird, getting an interesting picture in place of a dead body.

PAGE 101

the mated pairs of the birds have flocked together: In domestic geese the mated pairs often live together for life; and among the wild geese this, doubtless, is often true.

PAGE 102

may I be awake to hear you: In what sense "awake"?

The wild geese are passing—southward: the end of the autumn, the sign that winter is here.